The
SHAGGY D.A.

The Shaggy D.A.

by

Vic Crume

From
Walt Disney Productions'
New Motion Picture
Screenplay by
Don Tait
© 1976 Walt Disney Productions

A FAWCETT GOLD MEDAL BOOK

Fawcett Publications, Inc., Greenwich, Connecticut

1

RETIRED ADMIRAL Gordon C. Brenner sat on his porch, longing for the feel of a rolling deck beneath his feet and a view of the broad Pacific, instead of the shady lawn.

Suddenly his blue eyes were alerted to the sight of a moving van rumbling up the street. It slowed, swung around, and backed into the Danielses' driveway next door.

"Movers. That's odd," he muttered. "Wilby Daniels never said a word about leaving Medfield. I thought they'd just gone for the weekend."

He watched as two men clad in white coveralls jumped down from the cab. "Wilby and Betty shouldn't have left a thing like this to the movers. Ten to one they'll forget to pack something."

But because the Danielses were young and nice at the same time, the admiral did his best to see that the movers stowed the Danielses' gear with care. He kept a sharp eye on the two men as they sped back and forth emptying the contents of his neighbors' house.

"Good work," he decided. "Everything shipshape."

One of the movers called out from the porch steps. "That's about it, Freddie?"

"It's gonna have to be, Dip," the other called back. "I can just about get this coffee table in."

The words coffee table gave Admiral Brenner a kindly idea. The day was hot. How about a cooling drink for the crew? He strode to the driveway.

"Lay to for a while men, and hoist one with me," he bellowed. "Lemonade. Back in a moment." He marched into his house.

Freddie and Dip exchanged glances. "Lemonade?" Dip mopped his forehead. "Think we'd better?"

"Why not?" Freddie shrugged. "Anything with ice in it. But we can't hang around long."

Almost immediately, the admiral returned carrying a tray. On it teetered three glasses and a pitcher of lemonade. He strode to the van.

"Thanks, Captain," Freddie grinned, reaching for a glass.

"*Admiral*. Gordon C. Brenner, Retired," the admiral corrected him quickly.

Dip shook his head. "Admiral! Say, Freddie—

you ever think we'd see the day an admiral would be bringing us a drink? Thanks, sir."

Admiral Brenner took a hearty swig and lowered his glass. "Don't make a practice of drinking with dock-wallopers," he said graciously, "but you lads have been working hard. You've earned it."

Dip crashed his molars up and down on an ice cube. "Great ice you got here, Admiral," he said noisily.

"Yeah," Freddie added. "Cooling."

The Admiral leaned against the back of the van. "So the Danielses are really weighing anchor, leaving town after all these years?"

"Guess so," Freddie replied.

"Fine neighbors. Nice people to lay alongside of. And I'll miss that young Brian. That's their boy— about nine or ten, I should say. Wilby has a nice law practice here in town. Can't help wondering why he'd leave."

"Lawyer, you said?" Dip asked sharply.

"Lawyer," the admiral repeated. "Do you know where they're putting down new anchorage?"

Before Dip could reply, Freddie broke in. "Say, Dip, we'd better be weighing anchor ourselves. It's getting late. Thanks for the drink, Admiral."

"Not at all," Admiral Brenner replied. "Just put the glasses here on the tray."

The movers hopped up into the cab, and turned the van into the street.

"Well done, lads!" The admiral waved the tray in a "goodbye" motion. Then, every inch a naval officer, he stepped back to his mailbox, labeled, THE FLAGSHIP. ADM. G. C. BRENNER RTD.

"Maneuver successfully completed. Funny the Danielses didn't bother to say goodbye. Oh well— ships that pass in the night, I guess."

There was no reason for Wilby Daniels, whom some readers may remember for his adventures with a shaggy dog, or his wife, Betty, or son Brian to notice the big van that passed them. No ESP warned them that almost all their worldly goods were speeding out of their lives.

Betty Daniels happily stroked the fur coat slung over the seat between herself and her husband. She smiled. "Thanks again for this coat, Wilby," she said smilingly. "It's just beautiful." She leaned her head back—but only for a moment. "Where on earth is that rock music coming from?" Quickly she turned to Brian, her ten-year-old son, sitting alone and content on the back seat. The rabbit-ear antennas of his transistor waved wildly to the motion of his mop of brown hair and the beat of the music.

"Brian! Will you turn that thing off before you deafen yourself?"

Brian bobbed the rabbit ears. "What?" he shouted.

His mother reached back and pulled the earphones from his head. "Turn that thing *Off*," she shrieked over the sudden blast of sound.

Brian snapped the switch. "Okay. It's off. Now what am I supposed to do?"

"Sit there! For goodness' sake, Brian, you can do it—we're nearly home."

Brian sat—about thirty seconds. He leaned forward. "Dad, I bet you a quarter you don't know how many eyes a fly has."

Wilby Daniels gave his golf cap a tug. "I'm a lawyer, not an entomologist."

"Well, take a guess," Brian urged.

"Two."

"*Two*?" They have thousands! Thousands of six-sided facets, each an eye in itself. You owe me a quarter, Dad. And what's an entomologist?"

"Take a guess."

Instead, Brian changed the subject. "Mom, how long do you think the longest apple peel in the world was?"

His mother sighed. "Brian, *please!*"

"Just guess."

Betty yawned. "Five feet."

"Wrong. Dad, what's your guess?"

"Brian, how could I *possibly* know? Never baked a pie in my life." Wilby slowed the car and swung into their driveway. "Home," he sighed. "Home at last."

In top shape for a man pushing forty, he hopped out of the car and reached in the back for his golf clubs. Betty got out, clutching her beautiful new coat. Brian, his mind still on apple-peel records, followed closely behind. "You should *try* a guess, Dad," he insisted, as his father fitted the key in the front door lock. "Say *something!*"

Wilby Daniels swunk open the door, took one look inside, and said something.

"WE'VE BEEN ROBBED!"

2

BETTY DANIELS peered around her husband's shoulder. Not a drape hung from a window. All that was left of their living room was wallpaper. "I don't believe it," she gasped.

Brian sped ahead of his parents and galloped to the kitchen. "You gotta believe it, Mom," he yelled back. "If you don't, come out here and see where the refrigerator used to be."

Wilby and Betty raced toward the back of the house. At the kitchen door, Wilby had won by a nose. He gulped. "I can't bear to see more!"

"See *more*, Dad? It's *less*. Even the telephone's gone."

"Betty," Wilby said, "you check upstairs. I've got to call the police. I'll go over to Admiral Brenner's and use his phone." He rushed out.

Searching wildly for the admiral's doorbell, Wilby wasted a moment or so before he remembered that the admiral had a ship's bell hung for that very purpose. He gave it a swift *clang*, and almost instantly the door opened.

"Why, Daniels! This is a pleasure. I suppose you came to say goodbye?"

Wilby stared. "Goodbye? I just got here. Admiral, may I use your phone? Mine's gone. I have to call the police. I've been robbed."

"Is that so? Well, well! At any rate, I hope you have smooth sailing in your new job, Wilby."

Wilby stared even harder. "Maybe I've cracked up. Maybe none of this is happening," he thought. He blinked his eyes rapidly. The admiral was still there, and looking unusually calm for one who had just been told of a robbery next door. "Admiral," he began slowly, "what was that you said about a new job?"

An equally strange stare came into the admiral's blue eyes. "And what was that you said about being *robbed*?"

Maybe the admiral had been dreaming, too. Wilby tried again. "We were robbed. Wiped out. Cleaned out. Didn't you see anybody over there?"

The admiral shook his head. "Nobody but the—" His jaw dropped.

"But the who?" Wilby asked sharply.

"But the movers," the admiral answered weakly.

"Movers!" It was no dream! Wilby dropped the phone book he had just picked up. "What movers? How long ago?"

The admiral frowned. "Now let me see. It was

a Sanderson Van and Storage outfit, I believe. And they came about two bells. Or maybe it was three bells."

Wilby rolled his eyes toward the ceiling. "How much are two bells? I mean how many? I mean— oh never mind. Let me just tell the police."

Pushing buttons rapidly, he concentrated on his call. "This is Wilby Daniels. My house has been robbed. Cleaned out. Yes."

The desk sergeant was not as excited about this news as Wilby. His voice quacked back. "I'm working one call now, and I have two on hold. Can you call back when we're not so busy?"

Wilby nearly climbed into the telephone. "But my house has been robbed. R-o-b-b-e-d. Robbed!"

"Those things happen." The sergeant replied calmly. "Don't act like the sky's fallen on your head. Hold the line. Got another call coming in."

Wilby shook the phone in rage. He glared over at the admiral. "This town is being systematically ripped off. And do you know why, Admiral?"

Admiral Brenner took a deep breath which he intended to use for giving an opinion. But Wilby beat him to the punch.

"Because when one of these thieves is caught, he's out on the street the next day doing business as usual. And do you know at whose doorstep I lay that?"

The admiral took another deep breath—too deep and too long. Wilby went blaring on. "That's right. Our own district attorney, Honest John Slade. *Honest* John! Ha! If *I* were the D.A. I'd prosecute to the fullest extent of the law. And I'd get *convictions*."

Behind him came a burst of applause. He turned to see Betty and Brian at the doorway. A slightly silly look came over his face. He put down the receiver. "I didn't mean to get up on my soap box," he said sheepishly.

Betty rushed up, beaming with pride at Wilby's fighting words. Her cute face now had an angry expression. "Never get down from it, dear. You look good. *Run* for district attorney!"

"You could catch all those criminals," Brian beamed. "Just like on TV."

"Well—er—well, if it weren't for my law practice I just might," Wilby said bravely.

"You could get your partner to cover that," Betty said eagerly. "And I'll be your campaign manager. My talents aren't limited to eggs over easy, dear. Try me."

"And I'll paste your face all over the city, Dad," Brian offered generously. "There won't be a telephone pole in Medfield I'll miss."

Admiral Brenner went sailing across the room where a ship's wheel was set into the fireplace wall. "And I'll be your fund-raising chairman, Wilby. I'll start the ball rolling right now—with a quarter." He began to spin the big wheel that worked the combination of his wall safe.

"Whoa, whoa there, Admiral," Wilby called out nervously. "I appreciate your good intentions *and* your quarter, but . . . but, well, let's sleep on it."

Betty sighed. "That's about all we will be sleeping on. We don't have beds."

Brian's face went gloomy. "Aw, Dad! I thought you wanted action—not sleep."

Firmly, Wilby led the family to the door. "Thanks, anyhow, Admiral. See you tomorrow."

The Danielses trailed homeward. Betty took the lead and looked neither left nor right. "Of course, Wilby, if you'd rather 'curse the darkness than light one little candle'—well, that's up to you. Come, Brian."

Wilby fell back a step or two. He looked at his two nearest and dearest stomping coldly ahead of him. "First my furniture, then my family," he muttered. "What more can a guy lose?"

Plenty! The night wasn't over!

Moonlight streamed across the bare bedroom and cast a silvery glow over Betty's fur coat. Huddled beneath it, the Danielses were sound asleep. Across the hall, Brian slept just as soundly under an assortment of family sweaters and Wilby's trench coat. All were blissfully unaware that, except for Brian's transistor set, their remaining possessions were about to disappear into the unknown.

Gloved hands reached into the closet. Wilby's golf clubs and trousers appeared. Next came Betty's clothes. Then gently, gently, the gloved hands reached down for the fur coat and carefully removed it from the sleeping pair.

Only minutes later, the same gloved hands were on the steering wheel of Wilby's car. As it purred off down the driveway, Wilby stirred in his sleep. He groped for the fur coat. No luck. Sleepily, he sat up and looked around. Instantly, he was wide awake.

"Betty! Wake up!" He shook her shoulder. "They hit us again! They stripped us right to the bone, while we were sleeping!"

Betty opened one eye. "Stripped us to the bone?" she asked sleepily. She felt her ribs. "No, Wilby. Stop dreaming. I have my slip on."

"Betty—wake *up*. You check on Brian. I'm going over to the admiral's. Got to use his phone and get the police."

Betty yawned. "Good luck with *that*, dear." She opened both eyes and sat up. *"Wilby! Where is my coat?"*

But Wilby was already leaping down the stairs. She went to the closet. "Oh, no! Wait'll Wilby finds out his golf clubs are gone! This town is going to see *action!*"

Wilby clanged the ship's bell back and forth. Lights turned on inside and the admiral's hearty bellow rang out. "Belay that or I'll—" He swung open the door and beheld Wilby's unusual street wear. "Wilby! What's the trouble, lad?"

Wilby rushed past him. "Got to use your phone."

The admiral listened as Wilby once more talked excitedly to the police. "Yes. My house has been robbed again. Again. Yes. I think I have an account with you. Yes. Daniels. D-a-n-i-e-l-s. And it's a name you'd better remember, because it's the name of the next district attorney in this city." He slammed down the receiver just as a wild cheer sounded.

"YEE-ay, D.A.!"

Wilby swung around to see Betty, all dressed up in her satin slip and his sweater. She was clapping madly. Brian, clad in boxer shorts, hopped up and down beside her. "Go get 'em, Dad. It's Victor-EE with W. D. I made that up just now!"

"Win with Wilby!" Betty cheered, rushing forward.

The admiral, carried away with excitement, shouted, " 'Damn the torpedoes. Full speed ahead!' " And for the second time within a few hours, he sailed across the room to his wall safe. But there was no need to give the ship's wheel a spin. The safe door was already open.

With a roar that could have blown a typhoon to a new course, the admiral turned to the Danielses. "Those dock pirates! They got me, too. I've been robbed!"

"And I could have used that quarter, too!" Wilby said angrily.

"Don't you worry, Wilby. We'll get funds. Just you concentrate on getting elected."

"In green-striped shorts?" Wilby looked down at his entire wardrobe. "How'm I going to get started?"

3

GETTING STARTED was not as hard as Wilby had thought it would be. By noon, with the admiral's help, he had all the neighbors' votes and some of their clothes as well. Medfield's Rent-All Furniture Company supplied the Danielses with some sorely needed household accessories, and the telephone company replaced their stolen telephone. By the end of the week, the bank, Wilby's theft insurance policy, and the admiral's money-raising efforts put the entire Daniels family hard at work on Wilby's campaign.

He picked Saturday as Supermarket Day. By only ten in the morning, his smile had frozen into position as he kept on handing out circulars and greeting shoppers both coming and going.

Betty pulled up in front of the market in the

rented campaign car. She got out and hurried to Wilby. "Here are more leaflets and a new broom, Wilby," she said.

He looked up smiling—as usual—and started to shake her hand. "My name is Wilby Daniels, young lady," he said. "I'd certainly appreciate your vote in the upcoming—" He stared at his wife of eleven years and dropped her hand. "Oh, it's you. Honestly, Betty, my hand is already sore and my smile is getting a permanent press."

"Your smile is charming and sincere," Betty assured him. "Keep it up. That's the technique that got me, remember?" She handed him the fresh supply of leaflets and the broom.

"What's the broom for?" he asked.

"A symbol of the new broom that's going to clean up this town, dear."

Wilby eyed it doubtfully. "I'm running for district attorney, not janitor. What'll I do with it?"

"Wag it now and then. *Ssh!*" she lowered her voice. "Here comes a customer for you. I have to run. And Wilby—don't forget to kiss that baby. It's more or less expected."

Wilby turned to see a very fat parent wheeling a pushcart full of groceries. Squeezed into the back was a large baby who matched his mother, dimple for dimple. He gazed over a waving celery stalk and viewed the world like a king viewing his realm. To add to his regal appearance, he even wore the royal purple—in the form of grape jelly.

Wilby's smile came unstuck. "Peanut butter and grape jelly. I can't do it!" he groaned. "It'd be like kissing a sandwich."

But a vote was a vote. He handed the mother a leaflet. "My! That is a beautiful baby, ma'am," he beamed, and bent slightly, searching for a dry spot on the baby's head.

"Why, thank you," the baby's mother said happily. "Joey, say hello to the nice man."

No one could say Wilby didn't have voter-appeal. Joey bounced himself upward, gave Wilby a loving smack, followed by a campaign contribution of one peanut butter and grape jelly sandwich—right in the kisser.

"*Joey!*"

"No problem. No problem," Wilby said, mopping up as fast as he could. "Lovely child, ma'am."

"You're a wonderful man, sir," she replied. "And you'd certainly get my vote—but I'm not registered."

Somewhere behind him a voice called out, "This way, please, Mr. Daniels."

Wilby turned to a blinding flash of a camera.

"Thank you, Mr. Daniels," said the news photographer, "just in time for the late afternoon edition!"

It certainly was! Brian Daniels picked up the Medfield *Bugle* from the front lawn. "Gosh!" he gasped, and went charging into the house to show his mother the front page photo of the head of the household. "Looks like mud on his face, Mom." He shook his head.

Betty gave it one horrified stare. "It's a smear campaign! I'll bet Slade is behind this."

Brian peered again at the photo. "I sure don't see him."

"Well, let's hope that picture won't be on the TV news. It would ruin your father's dinner."

Over at the D. A.'s office, Honest John Slade, laughing his head off, slapped the *Bugle* down on his desk. He read the headline aloud to the group of newspaper reporters crowding the room. *"Unknown Pledges Dynamic Campaign Against Slade."* He chuckled. "And he's going to clean up the city! Well, boys, looks to me as though he'd better clean himself up first."

Everybody laughed, but no one laughed quite so hard as Raymond, the D. A.'s assistant. Still guffawing, he pointed to one of the reporters. "Your question, now."

The reporter took a forward step. "How do you feel about Daniels' charges that you're failing to go after criminals in Medfield, Mr. Slade?"

Honest John leaned back comfortably. "Typical election stuff. He's trying to grab space in the news. But I know you people are too smart to fall for that."

A light flashed softly on his desk and Honest John swiftly flashed a sharp look at his assistant at almost the same moment. Right away, Raymond turned to the reporters. "That's all Mr. Slade has time for right now, ladies and gentlemen. There are refreshments in the next room. I'll lead the way."

Slade waited until the door closed, then opened a desk drawer and lifted out a telephone. "Yes,

Eddie," he said in a low voice. "Got it right in front of me. Nothing to worry about."

At the other end of the D. A.'s hotline, Eddie Roschak, the crime boss of the entire county, scowled. "Well, I don't like these crusading candidates, Slade."

"Eddie, believe me. The guy's a lightweight. He'll fade in the stretch."

"I hope you're right," Roschak replied coldly, chomping his cigar.

"Eddie, don't worry. You just take care of things over there in the warehouse. Leave this end to me." He hung up.

The Slade-Daniels race might have been just one more in Medfield's political history if Freddie and Dip, the two "movers," hadn't decided to take an afternoon off for cultural interests. They strolled through the door of Medfield's proudest building, the Prescott Museum.

Dip, never a one to overlook the chance of making a little money, nudged Freddie. "Remember, this place has all kinds of old junk. If you spot something, leave the job to me. Understand?"

"Sure do. Nobody can scoop it up without anyone seeing like you can. Where do we start?"

Dip looked around. "We want to get into a group. You know—where some guy is explaining something. We can be with them but not *looking* with them. Understand?"

"Sure do. Look over there, Dip. Isn't that a group shaping up around that professor-type guy?"

"You got it! Let's go."

Giant-size oil paintings were not objects Dip could scoop up, no matter how clever he was. And it was not until their guide, Professor Whatley, reached a painting of a woman smiling pleasantly down upon a snarling shaggy dog that Dip and Freddie got interested in the tour they had joined.

"What's she smiling about?" Freddie asked. "Looks like that dog is planning to tear her apart."

Other members of the group nodded, and agreed that the artist had chosen an unreal situation to paint.

Professor Whatley smiled. "That is exactly what all of our visitors think when viewing this remarkable painting. It does demand explanation. You have all heard of the famous Borgia family in your study of history, I presume. This painting shows a member of that family so famous for poisoning their enemies—Lucrezia Borgia. Legend has it that Lucrezia once transformed an unfaithful suitor into a dog. Not by poison, in this case. In this painting, Lucrezia is supposed to have used the ring on her finger for revenge. If you notice closely, the ring she wears is identical to the one we have displayed here in this case."

He moved over to a glass display case and pointed to a strange-looking piece of jewelry.

"Looks like a bug to me," Freddie said.

The professor nodded. "It's a scarab—a member of the *scarabaeid* beetle family. The Egyptians wore them as talismans. If you'll note, this scarab seems to glow, then fade, then glow."

Freddie laughed loudly. "Maybe it's supposed to be a lightning bug."

Professor Whatley's voice became chilly. "To continue—. Again, according to legend, Lucrezia's powers of transmutation—that is, in this case, the power of changing the man into a dog—stemmed from this very ring."

Dip snickered. "Trans*mutt*ation."

The professor glared. "The museum has put added safeguards on this display. Several years ago an incident occurred that defied scientific explanation."

Dip quickly posed a question to head off any long scientific explanation the Professor might dream up. "Is it valuable?" he asked.

Professor Whatley sighed deeply. "It would be impossible to estimate its value. The ring is priceless." He glanced at his watch. "We must move along, I fear. Closing time is almost upon us."

Freddie tagged along with the group into the next room. He glanced back in time to see Dip carefully close a side slot in the display case. He shook his head. "That Dip! What a partner! Special safeguards and it took him two seconds to get the goods!"

It was well after dark before Freddie and Dip rang Boss Roschak's private buzzer at the Medfield Storage and Supply warehouse. Their footsteps echoed as they walked on through the huge cavernlike building to the upstairs office at the end. On either side were neat lines of refrigerators, washing machines, dryers, TVs, and stereo-TV combinations, (Wilby's among them). Beyond those were neatly crated boxes stacked nearly ceiling high.

"Looks like the boss isn't getting much of a turnover," Dip whispered.

"Don't you worry about Eddie Roschak, Dip," his partner whispered back. "That guy knows what he's doing. Probably holding out for another rise in inflation before he sells."

"We'd better do the same thing when we show him the ring. You handle it, Freddie. You're good on talking."

Freddie chuckled. "And you're good on *taking*."

But in spite of the pair's talents, Eddie Roschak, a very tough crook, was not interested in their day's haul.

He tossed it down on the desk. "It's a piece of junk. Why didn't you bring me something I could use?"

"Junk!" Freddie exclaimed. "The fellow at the museum said it was priceless. Priceless is better even than costing a lot."

Dip bobbed his head. "Yeah. Priceless isn't *payless,* ya know. That's a lot of loot you got there in front of you. Some dame named Lucy Borga used to doll up with that ring."

"Lucrezia *Borgia*, Dip," Freddie said, showing off. He turned to Roschak. "It was her personal property. She wore it on state occasions."

Roschak looked again at the ring. It seemed to brighten and fade, brighten and fade. He rubbed his eyes and pushed it across the desk. "So who do I sell it to? Another museum? Diamond rings, emerald rings, those I can move."

"Make us an offer, Mr. Roschak," Freddie said.

"A grand," Dip added hurriedly.

Eddie Roschak waved his hand. "Get out of here!"

Dip leaned forward. "*Anything*, Mr. Roschak. Make an offer. We gotta make a living same as the next guy."

The Boss scowled. "Look. I'm tellin' ya. There's no call for bug rings. Now get lost, both of you."

Crime boss Eddie Roschak had just made the biggest mistake of his highly successful career!

4

BETTY DANIELS jumped up from the breakfast table and hurried her plate and coffee cup over to the sink. "No dawdling over coffee this morning, dear. The TV people said they'd probably be here around ten or so—and I've a million things to do."

"You won't have to dust the furniture, Mom," Brian said cheerfully. "That's one good thing about being robbed."

"That's right!" Betty exclaimed. "And another good thing is those apple crates we've put in the living room instead of renting furniture. They'll show Medfield voters that your father has experienced crime first-hand. He'll be the *ideal* man to vote in as D. A." She turned to Wilby. "Aren't we lucky, dear, that the TV station is doing its

"Meet Your Candidate" program right here at home? It's a wonderful chance for the voters to meet a nice average family. And I'm not planning to say too much about being your manager. That way, you'll get the women who aren't women's libbers. And yet my *being* your manager will bring in the women's lib vote."

"You'd get my vote, too, *if* I could vote, if you gave me a cost-of-living raise, Dad," Brian suggested.

"I will not offer bribes," Wilby replied sternly.

Brian shrugged. "Okay. But it's going to sound pretty funny on TV when I'm interviewed on my allowance."

"It'll sound great!" his mother exclaimed. "Voters will know you are a sensibly brought-up child."

Brian sighed. "I guess so. But couldn't you spare me a quarter, Dad? I could sure use it."

"Okay." Wilby fished a quarter from his pocket. "But remember—you're going to be on the program with us, so stick around the neighborhood this morning."

The greater part of Brian Daniels' allowance usually found its way into the hands of Tim, driver for Dolly Dixon Ice Cream and Pies. An extra quarter was just what Brian needed for his morning between-meal snack, and he was delighted to hear the sound of Tim's bell down at the end of the block.

Tim was one of Brian's favorite persons, although Tim didn't feel *exactly* the same way about Brian. Every time they met—which was often—Brian checked him out on the entire list of Dolly Dixon's forty-four flavors. This morning was no different. Tim had taken a deep breath when he saw Brian rolling towards him on a skateboard. Just as Brian reached him, Tim was nearing the end of his recitation. ". . . Gingerbread rocky road slush, kumquat Bavarian chocolate with lime mint, and pine-scented gooseberry," he finally finished.

"That's only forty-three," Brian replied.

"You sure?"

"I was counting."

Tim frowned. "Now what did I forget? Oh, yes. Avocado surprise. Well, what's it gonna be?"

"A vanilla ice cream sandwich."

Tim turned to Elwood, his large shaggy dog, who rode in the front seat with him. Elwood was man's best friend and Tim's super-best friend. "What do you think, Elwood? Brian's going to take a vanilla sandwich. Do you want one too?"

Even though Elwood's coat was so shaggy that his eyes were almost hidden, hopeful glints sparkled out, and he gave his tail a cheerful wag.

Tim held out a broken corner of a vanilla ice cream sandwich to Elwood, and handed Brian a Dolly Dixon Super-Colossal. "Don't break your neck on that skateboard, Brian," he advised. "I wouldn't want to lose a customer like you. It'd be like losing my check list."

"Okay. Guess it would be," Brian agreed. "Well, I gotta skate home now. My Dad's gonna be on TV." He adjusted his headset and antennas, slapped a picture of his father over the truck painting of Dolly Dixon, herself, and coasted off.

Tim sighed. "Elwood, if I have to go through all

those forty-four flavors again for that kid, I'll go banana nut."

Elwood nodded and leaped back up into the passenger seat. As the pair started off, a TV mobile truck pulled up at the Danielses' curb. "Look, Elwood! Must be that Mr. Daniels is going to be on one of those 'Meet Your Candidate' programs right there at home."

Elwood again nodded his shaggy head, and on they went in search of more customers around the block.

Brian skateboarded up to the curb. He watched with interest as the TV crew set up equipment, before he coasted right on into the living room.

"They want the place to have that barren, stark look showing the ravages of crime," the TV director was saying to the interviewer. "Daniels' wife is also his campaign manager, so keep the lid on her."

"Where is she now?"

"Upstairs getting ready, I guess."

Brian, still munching his ice cream sandwich and wearing his transistor set, skateboarded out from the doorway. Expertly, he curved in and around the cables stretched along the floor, and headed for the stairs.

"What was *that*?" asked the interviewer.

"Daniels' kid. Try to work him in some way. Maybe you could ask him about his allowance. Stuff like that. We want to have the family scene."

Brian clumped on up the stairs and entered his parents' room. His mother, practicing her speech and making faces before a rented mirror spotted him in the background. She turned to him in a graceful kind of way. "Hello, Brian, darling," she said softly.

Brian stared. "You changing your personality or something?" he asked.

"Why, darling! What an odd thing to—." Her voice suddenly changed to its everyday sound. "Hey! What's that you're eating?"

She swiftly plucked the remainder of the sandwich and tossed it into a wastebasket. "We don't eat junk between meals in this house."

Brian stared. "We don't? Since when?"

"Since we decided to become a prominent family in Medfield," his mother replied calmly. "No prominent families eat junk between meals."

"Do they get to eat it *at* meals, then?" Brian asked, eyeing the wastepaper basket sadly.

There was no reply, so he flung himself into a rented chair. "Some life!" he muttered as his father entered the room holding up two ties.

"Which of the admiral's ties do you like best, Betty—the navy blue or the navy blue?"

"The navy blue," Betty grinned. "And Brian, change your shirt."

Brian didn't stir. Wilby pulled the earphones from his son's head. "Change your—" Wilby stopped instantly when he heard out of the earphones, a newscaster's voice crackling "... stolen from the Prescott Museum. Exact value of the ring has not been determined. But Professor Whatley, the museum curator, said it was one of the museum's most valuable pieces."

"Work that into your speech on the show,

Wilby." Betty said quickly. "It will point up the fact that crime is—"

"*Ssh!*"

"Well, Wilby. Really! I *am* your campaign mana— Wilby! What's wrong!"

Wilby Daniels had turned pale. "That might have been the Borgia ring that was stolen."

"What's the Borgia ring?"

Wilby turned even paler. "The ring that turned me into a dog when I was a kid."

Betty's mouth opened—and closed. She glanced at Brian. He looked more interested than alarmed. "Maybe I just didn't hear right, Wilby. What did you say?"

"I said—" Wilby stopped. "Brian, why aren't you in school?"

"Because it's summer vacation."

"Then why aren't you straightening up your room?"

"Because there's nothing in it," Brian replied, not stirring from his chair.

"Well, why don't you get lost? And in case you plan to ask, *because I said so.*"

Not in the least surprised by this sentence of exile, Brian marched toward the door. He turned around. "Okay. Anything you say. But rejection will make me grow up to be inhibited and a non-achiever, and it'll be your fault." He closed the door behind him, then quietly opened it a crack. He listened.

"The day that kid is inhibited—"

"*Or* a non-achiever," his mother giggled. "He achieves something every third second! But go ahead, Wilby. What am I supposed to hear that Brian isn't supposed to hear?"

"I'm not sure that you'll understand." There was a long pause before he again spoke. "When I was a teenager, I accidentally took an old ring from the Prescott Museum. A wing caught on my sweater sleeve—that's how it happened."

Already Betty began to look as though she did not understand. "A wing on a *ring*, Wilby?"

He nodded. "A scarab beetle ring. There was a strange inscription inside the band."

"What did it say?"

"I'd rather not mention it. Anyhow, when I got home and found it there on my sleeve I read it out loud several times. You know—in a kind of singsongy way." He took a deep breath. "And *I was turning into a dog*."

"Oh, Wilby!"

"There was this big shaggy dog next door—and I *became that dog*."

Betty looked at him closely. "You're sure you're feeling all right?"

"See. You don't believe me. I'm sorry I told you."

"I'm glad you told me, honey," she patted his arm. "It's nothing really. Just all this tension."

Wilby moved away from her. "If someone reads that inscription aloud, I could be transformed into a dog again!" he groaned.

Betty's voice was carefully calm. "I like that blue tie on you, Wilby. It brings out the color of your eyes."

"Didn't you hear what I said?"

"Of course I heard, dear." She turned back to

the mirror. *"And we're just going to pretend you never said it."*

Wilby clapped a hand to his head and started toward the door. Brian scooted swiftly into his own room.

Over on Appleton Street, Freddie was missing his chance to meet his candidate on TV. He had also missed the news broadcast about the stolen ring. He had no way of knowing that even though Boss Roschak had turned it down, the ring really *was* priceless.

"Now, where'm I going to unload this bug?" he asked aloud. "Who'd want it?"

Almost as he asked this question, Tim came jingling up to the curb. "Did you ask me something, mister?" he called out to Freddie. Tim was always on the lookout for new customers.

Freddie stepped over to the truck. "Pardon me, sir," he began. "But may I have a moment of your time?"

"How about an ice cream sandwich, too? We call it the Super-Colossal," Tim told him helpfully.

"By all means. Vanilla will be splendid."

Munching the first delicious bite, Freddie sighed very sadly.

"Anything wrong?" Tim asked anxiously. "Our vanilla is one of our best sellers. Brian Daniels—he's one of my regulars—he gets them all the time."

"Goodness no. This sandwich is the finest one I've tasted since I left France."

"France? Is that so?"

Freddie managed another heavy sigh. "Alas, yes.

Will you allow me to introduce myself?"

"Sure."

Freddie bowed. "I am a professor from the University of France."

"I'm Tim," Tim said politely. He waved to the truck. "From Dolly Dixon's," he added.

Freddie bowed again. "I hate to tell anybody this, but I am in financial trouble. I'm forced to part with this family heirloom at only a part of its real value." He held out the scarab ring. "It's a princely relic—"

"I thought it was a ring," Tim said, examining the beetle ring closely.

"So it is," Freddie said. "I will part with it for the reason that I must raise some money."

Elwood turned the ring about. "Elwood, do you think Katrinka would like this ring?"

Elwood refused to make any comment, so Freddie hurried into the conversation. "Who is Katrinka?" he asked.

Tim blushed. "Katrinka Muggelberg. She's in the pie department of Dolly Dixon. She's also captain of the South Side Steam Rollers—just about the best jammer they've got."

"*Hmm*! A roller derby?" Freddie asked.

"Imagine you being from France and all, and knowing about roller derbies! Yes, that's Katrinka."

"I'm certain she'd fall in love with the ring," Freddie said, bowing again. No one could have imagined him dressed in white movers' coveralls at that moment. He looked very dignified—the sort of man who would think nothing of owning many valuable rings.

Tim hesitated. "I bet she *would* love it! How much is it?"

"Circumstances force me to sacrifice it at five hundred dollars," Freddie replied.

Instantly, Tim turned back to the truck. Katrinka would have to fall in love with an ice cream sandwich. The ring cost far too much.

Suddenly Freddie's voice changed completely to his white coverall accent. "Would you spring for five bucks, Mac?" he pleaded.

"That's a lot of ice cream sandwiches," Tim answered doubtfully.

"But think of Miss Muggelberg. She'll *love* it."

That was enough for Tim. One thought of Katrinka and his billfold almost leaped out of his pocket. "Okay, sold," he said.

Plain old Freddie the Mover had a deal!

5

WILBY SAT at his desk in the den, trying to put the Prescott Museum theft out of his mind, and the upcoming TV interview into it. He hoped the cameras wouldn't show he was bouncing like popcorn.

"Just be yourself, Mr. Daniels." The TV interviewer spoke calmly. "First, we'll ask your wife a few questions out in the living room. Then we'll bring the cameras in here—a sort of surprise-you-at-your-work idea, you know. You'll look up and take it from there."

"You'll be wonderful, Wilby," said Betty, "and you will be too, Brian. And don't worry. I'm not going to come over as a bossy campaign manager."

"You sure have been coming over as a bossy

mother," Brian said. "I could have used that ice cream sandwich."

"Bossy! Who, me? Hand me those lilies, Brian."

"*Lilies!*" Wilby, Brian, and the interviewer gasped almost together.

"Of course, lilies. They'll make me look very feminine." She draped them over her arm, and smiled gently.

"I like you better bossy, Mom," Brian frowned.

The director's voice came over the floor speaker. "Places, please," and Betty followed the interviewer into the living room.

From the van, the director looked toward the house. "Five . . . four . . . three . . . two . . . you're on the air."

Admiral Brenner, next door, settled back comfortably to watch "Meet Your Candidate." The interviewer smiled out at him from the screen. "We will be meeting Wilby Daniels and his family. Daniels is the man whom many feel is undertaking the impossible task of unseating long-established district attorney, John Slade."

"Impossible task!" the admiral glared. "We'll just see about that on election day!"

"And so," the interviewer continued, "we'll have to wait and see how it goes on election day."

The admiral leaned forward. "That's just what I got through telling you, you deck swab! Get on with it."

"And now we are about to meet Betty Daniels, the candidate's wife and also his campaign manager. Practical Mrs. Daniels is simply making the best of things with these apple crates you see here. But how hard it must be to find that thieves have stripped your home of valuable possessions!"

The cameras shifted to Betty. To the admiral's shock, she gazed sadly out at him over a bouquet of calla lilies. She looked as though she couldn't manage an apple crate, much less a hard-driving campaign.

"That's not the girl I know!" the admiral boomed aloud. "Are those TV people trying to wreck Wilby's career? She looks as though she's expecting to *bury* him!"

The interviewer, too, had the feeling that this was not the same brisk, young Mrs. Daniels he'd seen in the den only moments before. "Er—we understand you're Mr. Daniels' campaign manager in his bid for the office of the district attorney?"

Betty smiled and looked even sadder. She began to arrange the lilies in a milk bottle. "Yes, I felt that as a *woman* I should put my shoulder to the wheel alongside my husband. I *urged* him to fight. I, his wife, should be at his side through the dark corridor that lies ahead."

Dark corridor! The admiral squeezed his eyes shut. "That's enough now. Bring on the candidate!"

But the candidate was still in his den deciding how to begin his first TV speech. He practiced looking surprised. "Oh! Hi there. I'm Wilby Daniels, and I—" he stopped. "Brian, don't stare at me."

"I wasn't staring."

"Well, I *thought* you were. Now—Hello. I'd like to take the opportunity to introduce myself. I'm Wilby Daniels, and I'm running for district attorney of your city." He paused and looked at

Brian. "Maybe I should say, 'our city.' "

"Sure. Why not? You live here too," Brian reminded him. "It's yours as much as anybody's."

"You're right, Brian. Absolutely right!"

Over on Appleton Street, Tim sat in his truck admiring his newly purchased ring. He showed it to Elwood. "Do you think Katrinka will like it, Elwood?"

Elwood thumped his tail, and Tim went on studying the ring. "Say, Elwood—there's something written here. *In canis corpore transmuto.*' Wonder what that means, Elwood?"

Tim thought a moment. "Well, I'll just tell Katrinka it means 'I love you.' That ought to get her!"

He looked at the ring dreamily. "And I sure do love her. *In canis corpore transmuto. In canis corpore transmuto. In*—" His voice trailed off and he failed to notice his super-best friend Elwood's strange reaction to this chant. By the time he looked over at the passenger seat, Elwood had faded from view!

Back in the Danielses' living room, the interviewer was trying to make Betty Daniels fade from view. But she went on sweetly discussing her great love of poetry—not a subject the admiral believed would catch the ears of Medfield voters.

Still practicing in the den, Wilby stared straight ahead. "Fellow citizens," he began. "I'd like to take this opportunity to—"

"Dad," Brian interrupted.

"Brian, *please*—"

"I just thought you ought to know you're getting a little gray, Dad. It's kinda funny."

Wilby paled. In alarm, he pulled a small mirror from the desk drawer. Small tufts of gray hair were sprouting around his forehead and neck. "*The ring!*" he cried out in panic. "Somebody's got the ring!"

Brian stared. "My gosh! What's wrong?"

"I'm turning into a dog. That's what's wrong."

"You're kidding. Really?" Brian's voice was loaded with interest. "I thought you were putting Mom on."

"Well now maybe she'll believe me," Wilby replied despairingly.

In the living room, the interviewer leaped into the middle of Betty's opinions on oil painting. "That's very interesting, Mrs. Daniels. And now I'm sure our viewers would like to *meet the candidate*. Where is he now?"

"I believe he is in his study, studying," Betty answered in a soft, sad voice.

"Never saw such a funeral in my life," Admiral Brenner grunted at the TV. "Wilby, you're going to have to get out here. Show 'em you're not dead, lad!"

Wilby was not dead but he was certainly half-gone, and disappearing fast. In only a moment, Brian was staring down at a large *shaggy dog*.

He looked his father over carefully. "Say, Dad— you look just like Elwood!" he exclaimed in a pleased way.

"I *am* Elwood, son," Wilby replied shakily. "Elwood-Wilby, I guess."

Brian patted his father's nose. "Never mind, Dad. You're *normal*, anyway. I mean, it isn't as though you'd turned into a werewolf, or something."

Wilby jerked away. "Brian! Stop petting my nose! Remember—I'm your father!"

Hardly had he spoken those words than Betty came drifting through the doorway with the TV interviewer. "And now I'd like you to meet my hus—" She stopped so quickly that the interviewer stumbled into her shoulder blades. Brian and Elwood-Wilby stared back at them.

Next door, Admiral Brenner fumed. "Now how'd that silly dog get into this? Of all the mismanagement! What do those TV people think they're doing?"

He listened closely for a possible explanation, but Betty didn't seem the one who'd be able to tell him.

"Where's your father?" she snapped, her dreamy way of speaking suddenly gone.

"Uh—he had to go," Brian answered. At the same time, he made a tiny downward jab toward Elwood's head.

Betty stood stunned. Helpfully, the interviewer tried to come to the rescue. "Well, then," he said easily, "we'll meet Mr. Daniels later. This, I presume, is your son Brian, and the family dog?"

Betty didn't even hear the question. Her eyes fastened on Wilby unblinkingly.

"Mrs. Daniels, this *is* your son, Brian, and the family dog. Right?"

"Right," she answered weakly.

The interviewer struggled bravely on. "What is the dog's name?"

"Bowser," answered Betty.

"Elwood," answered Brian.

"Elwood," Betty said quickly.

"Bowser," Brian said, just as fast.

Out in the TV van, the director and a technician exchanged startled glances. "Say, what kind of a family is in there, anyhow?" the director asked.

"Phonies," his helper answered. "Bet they don't even own that dog. Didn't even know his name. Daniels probably borrowed him for voter-appeal—trying to get the animal lovers' votes."

Back in the den, the interviewer went slogging ahead. "My! He certainly is a nice-looking dog, Mrs. Daniels. Is he smart?"

Betty's voice wobbled. "Oh, I'd say so. He's certainly above the average."

Wilby looked up faintly pleased. He wagged his tail. But Brian looked down at his father doubtfully. "I don't know," he said unexpectedly. "He thought a fly had two eyes. Remember, Mom?"

The interviewer clutched the mike desperately. "What I mean is—can he do any tricks?"

"No!" Wilby growled.

The men in the van listened as Mrs. Daniels' voice came over. "I guess so." Brian's voice followed. "Sure." And for a second time, a distinct "No" was heard.

"Who said 'no,' " the director asked, puzzled.

"We're picking up a ghost somewhere," his technician replied. "Listen, here's the kid again."

"Come on, boy," they heard Brian say. "You can do it. I've seen you. Speak! Come on, boy. Speak!"

Wilby looked up hopelessly. "*Woof*," he said clearly.

"*Woof*!" the interviewer gasped. "He *did* speak."

"Oh, no!" Betty's voice rang out strongly. "He doesn't *really* speak. Maybe he's coming down with a cold. Usually, he goes, '*Wooooff*.' "

By this time, Admiral Brenner was just about to rise from his chair and march straight over to Wilby's house. "This is costing Wilby votes!" he exclaimed. "Get that stupid mutt out of there. I didn't put up my quarter for a bad dog act!" He glared at the screen.

The interviewer wasn't happy either. "Can your dog sit up?"

"No way!" Wilby muttered.

Brian rushed between his father and the camera. "We'll help you, Elwood," he said. "Mom, grab his other hand. I'll take this one."

Betty, still stunned, reached for a shaggy paw. Together, they hauled Wilby into a sitting position, then dropped his paws. Over went Wilby thumping his shaggy head on a corner of the desk. "OUCH!"

"That dog *said*, 'ouch!' " the interviewer gasped.

Admiral Brenner could stand no more of such nonsense. He leaped to his feet and yelled at the TV. I've had enough of this!" Snapping the switch, he went pounding out to pace his front porch.

Wilby had had enough too, and when Tim's

whistle sounded from outdoors, Wilby lumbered to his four paws.

"Elwood! Where are you, Elwood?" came Tim's cry.

Wilby clumped over to the window and put his front paws on the sill.

Tim rushed across the lawn. "Why, Elwood! That's not your house!"

"Oh, no?" Wilby muttered crossly. He left the window and started off at a good clip across the room to the kitchen door.

"Elwood! Come back here!" Betty, Brian, and Tim called out at once.

Wilby didn't give his wife and child a backward glance. As the camera followed his movements, he skidded across the kitchen floor. Then standing up and putting his paws on the doorknob, he turned it neatly and bolted out.

"Pretty smart for a dog, huh?" Brian beamed up at the interviewer.

There was no reply to this. Only a thankful voice, saying, "We'll return to 'Meet Your Candidate' after a brief message."

It was the best line the interviewer had had on the show.

6

WILBY'S one idea was to get away—forever, if possible. But it was not to be. First in his path as he galloped across the yard was Admiral Brenner. The admiral, tired of pacing the porch, was starting out for the Danielses' house.

Down went the admiral and away dashed shaggy Wilby.

"That brute!" the admiral bellowed, rolling to a sit-up position. "Dolly Dixon Ice Cream and Pies is certainly going to hear about *this*." *POW*! Hardly had he spoken than he was decked a second time. He gazed up from beneath a heavy weight and caught a glimpse of Tim's startled face. "On your feet, sailor!" he roared.

Tim lost no time in scrambling up, but not because a retired admiral had sung out the order.

It was the sight of Elwood aiming for a hiding place behind a flowering bush at the edge of the admiral's porch that made him race forward.

The admiral was hard at his heels. "Get out of my flower bed, you moulting rug!" he cried.

"Elwood! You come back here!" Tim dived smack into the bush. He clutched Elwood's shaggy shoulder. "What's gotten into you, Elwood?" he implored.

"Get out of my flower bed! And you too," the admiral shouted at Tim.

Wilby bounded out, dragging Tim right along with him—straight through the admiral's flowers. It was a fast and bumpy ride for Tim. In a shower of California golden poppy petals, he glimpsed the admiral's ankles as he rolled and twisted past. "Sorry. Just leaving, sir," he gasped.

Admiral Brenner's temper rose high as the moon. He shook his head. "If I catch you in my flowers again, it's a month in the brig for both of you."

Keeping a firm grip on the struggling Wilby, Tim staggered to his feet. "What's gotten into you, Elwood?" he asked again. "This is not like you. I think that man back there was upset."

Wilby refused to make any sort of reply, and Tim lifted him up to the passenger seat. "Elwood, don't you remember when you were just a little puppy in that box outside the market?"

Wilby shuddered. "What kind of nightmare am I in?" he muttered to himself. "I certainly don't remember ever being a little puppy!"

"Don't growl, Elwood," Tim said, stroking Wilby's head. "You were the scrawniest one in the litter. You were no bigger than a Dolly Dixon Ice Cream Sandwich Regular. I took you home in my pocket. Remember?"

Wilby looked Tim straight in the eye. "Let me go or I'll deck you."

"*Elwood*! After all I've done for you! What a terrible way to talk!"

Wilby turned his head and stared in the other direction. He didn't see Tim turn pale, or see him begin to blink rapidly. "*Elwood*." Tim's voice dropped to a whisper. "You *spoke* to me. *I've got a talking dog*! Elwood, how'd you *learn*?"

Wilby gave Tim a dirty look. "I started out with 'ga-ga,' then went on to 'din-din.' Same as you."

Tim gasped. "Same as me? Elwood, this is wonderful! I've got a talking dog!" He stared at his super-best friend. "Elwood, you've given me a terrific idea—something that will be good for both of us. You stick with me, and I'll make you as big as Rin Tin Tin and Lassie put together." His eyes rounded into circles as he thought of the future. "Tim and his Talking Dog! How's that sound?"

Wilby glared into the windshield. "Awful."

But Tim, already zooming into a glorious future, didn't hear. "We'll get our own show, Elwood. We'll make it big in Las Vegas. We'll make *millions*. One for you and four for me." He loosened his hold on Wilby and began counting on his fingers. "Now let me see—one for you and four for me and one for you and four for me and—"

Wilby stared in disgust. It was time to make a break for freedom. Anything would be better than watching Tim work his way through all ten fingers. He leaped down.

Cries followed as Tim came rushing after him. "Elwood! Elwood! Come back! Three for me and two for you. Okay? Stop running. Can't we at least sit down and talk about it?"

Wilby took a backward look. To his horror, Tim was gaining on him. "I can't let him get me or I'll be riding an ice cream truck the rest of my life. I'll only see Brian on sandwich days!" He whizzed around a corner and squeezed through a hedge into a neighbor's backyard.

"Elwood! Elwood!" Tim called pitifully. "Come back! I'm sure we can come to some agreement."

At the moment, Wilby was safe from Tim. But his troubles were far from over. A Great Dane came loping across the lawn snarling and barking. Speedily, Wilby backed up—back, back, and right into a large doghouse. The rightful owner charged into it. Wilby hastened to back out—not Elwood-Wilby but Wilby Daniels. "Nice doggie!" he said softly, brushing his pants leg. "Stay! Stay!"

For a second, "nice doggie" was too shocked to move. Wilby took quick advantage of this and hurried out on the sidewalk. The Great Dane, recovering, tore out after him. Wilby glanced down the street. Tim's truck was still parked by the curb. In the passenger seat, yawning his head off, was shaggy Elwood.

Wilby headed for home, heels flying.

On his front lawn, the TV people were milling about, frantic. So was Wilby's wife. "I'm sure he'll be back any moment," she pleaded. "Can't you show another commercial?"

"I'm sorry, Mrs. Daniels. We've already shown eight commercials, two standbys, and a test pattern."

Brian's arm shot out. "There's Dad now!" he shouted. "Look, Mom! Look what's chasing him!"

"Places everybody!" the director yelled, and scrambled to the safety of the van.

The others raced into the house. "Run, Dad! Run!" Brian shouted.

"Places, everybody. Places! Swing the camera on the front door!"

It was the best "Meet the Candidate" show the TV station had ever filmed. Action! And what action! Wilby went panting into the living room. Brian slammed the door almost on the Great Dane's nose. "Whoa!" he yelled from the safe side of the living room door.

Wilby went whipping straight in front of the cameras. "Hi, there!" he gasped breathlessly. "I'm Wilby Daniels. And if I'm elected district attorney, I promise that I will bring order out of chaos. Or, in other words, I'll clean up Medfield. And I'll start by finding the links between crime boss, Eddie Roschak, and your present district attorney, John Slade."

Betty rushed to Wilby's arms. "Oh, Wilby! You're wonderful! You named *names*!"

Brian's eyes glowed. "I bet there isn't a kid in town with a dad like you!"

"Praise be," Wilby whispered. He grinned, and

swinging away from the cameras, gave each member of his family a big kiss.

Tim was too surprised to speak when he saw Elwood sitting calmly on the passenger seat. He started up the truck and headed for his friend Harry's business location, Harry's Corner—well named, as it belonged to Harry and was on the corner of Poppy and Palm.

"I want to give you some last minute advice before we go in, Elwood," he said. "This is going to be a good experience for you. It'll let you get used to talking before the public before we hit the big time. Come on, now."

Never before had Elwood been invited to step along into Harry's Corner. He wagged his tail and looked pleased.

"Keep mum, Elwood," Tim warned. "I don't want to blow this."

In they went. Tim smiled. "Hey, Harry. How's it going, ol' buddy?"

Harry began to smile, saw Elwood, and shook his head. "No dogs, Tim. You know that."

Tim grinned. "Sure, Harry, I know that. But this is no dog."

Harry took a closer look. "Yeah? What is it?"

"It's a *talking* dog," Tim said proudly. "Smart as anybody in this room."

"Out!" said Harry sternly.

"Five bucks says my dog can talk as good as you or me." Tim smacked five dollars down on the counter and grinned at all Harry's customers.

Harry shrugged. "Tim, keep your money. Look—

how about a nice cool glass of water? It'll be on the house."

Tim bent double laughing. "Chicken!" he exclaimed. "Forget it, Harry. My dog, Elwood, will now give you a chorus of 'Mary Had a Little Lamb.' I think we all know that one. Take it away, Elwood!"

Elwood yawned and stretched out on the floor.

Tim frowned. "Come on, Elwood. I'll help you get started. 'Ma-ary ha-ad—,' remember?"

Elwood merely thumped his tail.

"Okay, Elwood," Tim said. "That was kind of a tough one. Tell 'em what you told me—how you used to ask for dinner. Din-din? Elwood—come on, *please!*"

Elwood contented himself with scratching a flea.

"Out!" Harry was even sterner than before.

Elwood got up and headed for the door. "See that?" Tim looked excited. "He heard every word you said. He'd have talked if he'd been in the mood."

"Out."

"I heard you," Tim replied coldly. "*Good*bye!"

Over at the warehouse, Eddie Roschak angrily switched off his TV set and punched out Honest John Slade's private number. "I don't like it, Slade," he growled. "He's coming on awful strong. He named names. *I don't like it.*"

Slade's voice crackled back. "Eddie, I'm telling you. There's nothing to worry about. Absolutely nothing."

"*You're* telling *me*! Well let me tell you, Slade,

if that guy gets elected, we're in trouble. *Both* of us." He slammed down the phone.

Slade turned to his assistant, Raymond. "Maybe Daniels could use a little mud on him. Get something on him, Raymond. Everybody's got a skeleton in the closet. Find his."

"Okay, boss. You say 'mud,' he'll get it."

The TV people gone, Brian watched his parents collapse on a pair of apple crates.

"This thing is serious, Betty. As long as that ring is floating around, someone will read that *In Canis Corpore Transmuto* stuff. I'll turn into a shaggy dog again. And who knows when that'll happen?"

"Maybe when you're taking the oath of office, Dad," Brian suggested helpfully. "That'd be a crack-up, wouldn't it?" His giggle froze as his parents stared at him. "Well, it was just an idea," he said, thumping his heel on the bare floor.

"Some idea," Wilby grunted.

"Wilby, we have to solve this problem," Betty frowned. "We can't go through life never knowing when you might turn into Elwood. As your campaign manager, I say we *have* to find that ring— and fast."

"Where would you start looking for a hot ring, Pop?" Brian asked. "I'll help. Just give me a clue."

There was a loud knock at the front door. Admiral Brenner swept in. He wasted no time. "Wilby, after that ridiculous TV show, I'm here to make sure you don't run out in the middle of the meeting tomorrow."

"What meeting?" Wilby's campaign manager asked.

"Look alive, girl!" the admiral roared. "You arranged it. Wilby is to be the guest speaker at the Daisies luncheon tomorrow. It may mean the women's vote for him."

Betty sprang up. "I completely forgot—and here I'm the president! Thank goodness you stopped by, Admiral."

She turned to Wilby. "We'll have to begin our search day after tomorrow, Wilby."

"What search?" asked the Admiral. "If you're trying to spot that ice cream dog, he's back on the truck. I saw him. *And he'd better stay there.* Now, remember—eight bells. See you tomorrow." He strode off.

"What's eight bells, Wilby?" Betty asked.

Wilby sighed. "I don't know. Either we've got to learn bells or the admiral's got to learn clock."

"Bet you'll be learning bells," Brian grinned. "Ding! Ding!"

7

BETTY DANIELS, wearing a large floppy-brimmed garden hat, looked around the huge U-shaped table at the members and guests of the Daisies, Medfield's garden club.

"It's a wonderful turnout, Wilby," she whispered to her husband. "You can have all the Daisies right in your pocket by the time you finish your speech."

"I wish the daisy on my shoulder was in my pocket," Wilby muttered back. "It's as big as a sunflower and it's tickling my ear. Why'd you have to have such big ones made?"

"Nonsense, Wilby! Who'd see a little daisy? It looks lovely on you. Admiral Brenner isn't complaining about his. Why should you?"

"He looks silly, and so do I," Wilby replied. "But

he doesn't have to stand up in front of everybody and make a speech."

Betty refused to say more. She glanced down at her notes, then smilingly arose, her wavy hat brim flopping gracefully as she did so.

Members and guests pushed back their dessert plates and coffee cups and settled down to hear the guest speaker.

Betty beamed at one and all. "I feel especially honored this afternoon to introduce our guest speaker—our Daisy-of-the-Day."

A polite titter swept along the U-shaped table. Wilby smiled bravely, twiddled his reading glasses, and tittered back as Betty went on . . . and on.

". . . and so I give you a man dedicated to the task before him. Mr. Wilby Daniels!"

A solid round of hand-clapping burst out as Wilby blushingly stood up and slipped on his reading glasses.

Out in the hotel lobby, Slade's assistant, Raymond, looked away from the bulletin board he was checking. "Huh! So Daniels is in there nailing down the Daisies vote. Big stuff. Wait'll he reads this!"

His glance went back to the bulletin board.

HONEST JOHN SLADE'S
ANNUAL CHERRY PIE FESTIVAL
Sponsored by John Slade
for
District Attorney Finance Committee
AUCTION!

Raymond chuckled. "We'll bring out the pies and take in the dough!"

But as he said those words, it was Katrinka

Muggelberg who was actually bringing out the pies. Over at the Dolly Dixon Ice Cream and Pies factory, several blocks from the hotel, she elbowed open the swinging doors of the loading area. Tim's truck was parked at the platform and he rushed forward to take the stacked trays from her powerful arms.

"Katrinka, you look just like a nurse—dressed all in white that way! And even your beautiful hair tucked under that white thing on your head. Just like an operating room nurse!" He gazed at her lovingly.

Katrinka merely lifted the clipboard from the top of the stacked trays. "We're outa kumquat and guava custard, but the rest is here. Sign this order."

Tim swung the trays into the truck then bent over the clipboard to obey Katrinka's instruction. "I got something for you, Katrinka," he said, blushing as he scribbled his initials.

Katrinka went over her checklist again. "Yeah? If it's another pine-needle-pillow-souvenir from somewhere, you can keep it."

"Oh, no! It's a ring!" Tim spoke proudly.

Katrinka looked up from the clipboard and sighed. "Look, Jim—"

"Tim," he said quickly.

"Yeah, Tim. Just because I waved at you one night at the roller derby—"

Tim interrupted. "You're the best skater the Steam Rollers got, Katrinka."

"Yeah. I know. But like I say, just because I waved back at you don't mean it's ring time."

Tim gazed at his heroine. "It's just a present, Katrinka. Here."

Katrinka took one look and a laugh rang out between a wild cackle and a giant *ho-ho*. "Just what I've always wanted—a bug ring. Where's the Cracker Jack?"

Tim looked shocked. "That didn't come from any *box*, Katrinka. The man said it was very valuable."

"I bet," she chortled, turning away.

"I'm losing her," Tim thought wildly. "Wait!" he called. "Katrinka, wait! I got something to tell you."

Katrinka turned. "Yeah? As what?"

"Well, I can't tell you *everything*, but Elwood and me are gonna have our own show."

"Yeah?" Katrinka looked bored but she picked up the ring again. "What's this writing in here mean?" She read aloud, slowly at first, then gave it another couple of tries. " '*In Canis Corpore Transmuto.*' What's it mean?"

It was no time to say, as he had planned, "It means 'I love you.' "

"I'll tell you next time, Katrinka," he said instead.

"Yeah?" She laughed again. "You gotta go look it up, I guess?"

In the short conversation that followed, neither Tim nor Katrinka noticed Elwood on the passenger seat quietly vanish from sight.

Wilby's speech was going well. Burst after burst of clapping rang out, and Betty looked up at him, pride glowing in her eyes.

"So what can you, the voters, do about the terrible state of affairs in Medfield?" Wilby asked the Daisies.

Before one Daisy could tell, Betty's look of pride changed to one of horror. *Wilby's face was getting shaggy.* Not knowing this dreadful fact, Wilby touched the rims of his glasses, then looked calmly up from his notes. "Let me answer that question," he said firmly. "You can—"

His campaign manager sprang to her feet. She flung her arms around the Daisy-of-the-Day, her broad-brimmed garden hat hiding him from view. "Thank you, Mr. Daniels," she cried out loudly. "And now our song chairman will lead us in a chorus of the Daisy hymn."

"But I'm not through!" Wilby gasped, tugging at his campaign manager's arms.

"Yes you are, dear. Get lost!" she hissed, giving him a hard push downward.

Although more than surprised by the actions of their president, every Daisy loyally began singing. Before they'd reached the chorus, the very spit and image of Elwood was locked beneath the table by more pairs of legs than Wilby had ever noticed before at one time.

He took one horrified look at his paws and tried to put them where they wouldn't be resting on a Daisy's shoes. His search was not in vain, but as he hurried forward under the table, he forgot to keep his tail under control. It fanned gently against a Daisy leg. She stopped singing. "Why Mr. Cadbury!" she exclaimed to her luncheon guest. "How dare you!"

Mr. Cadbury also broke off mid-note as Wilby's tail gave him a brisk *thumpp*. He turned scarlet. "I never thought there'd be goings-on of this sort at a ladies luncheon," he thought in a confused rush of feeling. Suddenly, scream after scream and squeal after squeal rose to the very ceiling of the banquet room.

Admiral Brenner leaped to his feet. It was plain to him that some sort of enemy action was going on beneath the tablecloth. "Ladies!" he bellowed. "Be calm!"

At that instant, Wilby's tail gave *him* a good belt. Over went the admiral—decked again by his friend and neighbor!

"For a candidate who's promised to bring order out of chaos, I'm scoring zero," Wilby moaned. All the confusion above him was raising the temperature of his cool, legal brain. "I must get out of here!"

At top speed, he took the shortest route to the lobby doors. Out in the open, he leaped the two arms of the U-shaped table. Cups, saucers, coffee, frosting, flower petals, clattered, spilled, stuck, or drifted, according to the nature of each. Wilby left it all behind him and went skidding out to the lobby and straight into the revolving doors.

He leaped to his feet and pushed. Once out on the sidewalk, Wilby flung open the door of a taxi parked at the curb.

"Where to?" asked the driver, not looking back, but reaching over to the meter flag.

Wilby gave his home address, the flag flipped down, and off he rode—straight past Dolly Dixon

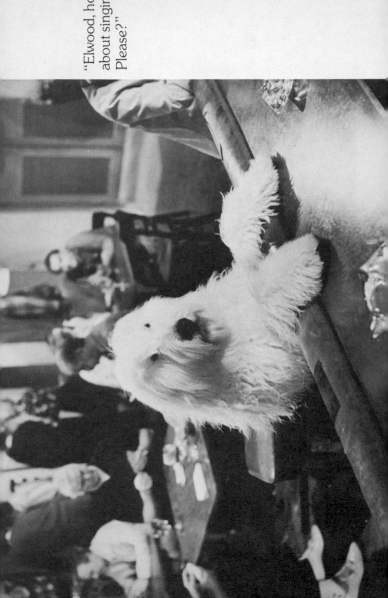

"Elwood, how about singing? Please?"

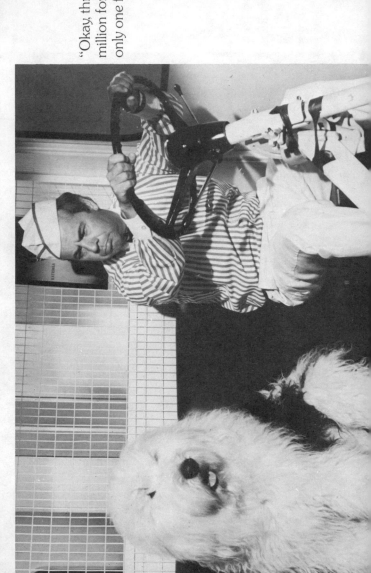

"Okay, three million for you — only one for me."

Wilby Daniels speaks before the Daisies.

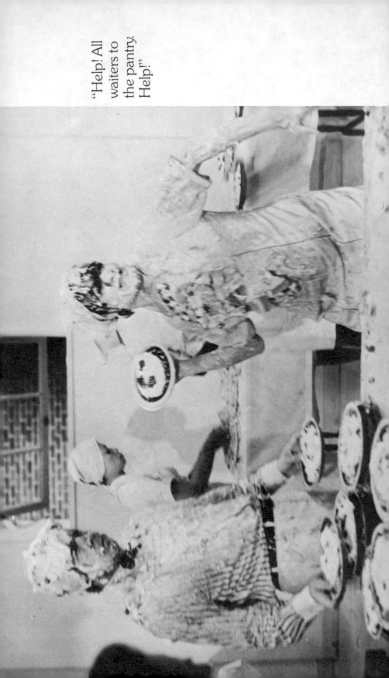

"Help! All waiters to the pantry. Help!"

"The Steam Rollers have fielded a new Skater...."

"In Canis Corpore Transmuto"

"How'd that dog get in here? Get him!"

"I love you" —Wilby.

headquarters. And just in time to give Tim a brief glimpse of the vanished Elwood riding at ease on somebody else's passenger seat!

"Elwood! Elwood!" he shouted, sprinting after the cab. "Why are you taking a taxi?"

At a red light up ahead, the driver kept his eyes on the signal for the change to green. "Who do you like in the election?" he called back to his customer.

"Daniels," Wilby answered promptly.

"I'm with you," the driver slapped the steering wheel. "But he ain't got a chance against the Slade machine."

Tim came galloping up, panting. He opened the cab door. "Come out of there, Elwood. Where were you going, anyhow?"

"Beat it!" Wilby growled.

Tim snapped on Elwood's collar and leash. He reached for Wilby's glasses and put them in his shirt pocket. "You didn't think you could fool me hiding behind those glasses, did you?"

"Watch it!" Wilby snapped. "Those are my reading glasses."

Tim hauled Wilby out the door and into the street, leaving a stunned driver staring into the rear-view mirror for a last glimpse of his remarkable passenger. Dazed, he moved forward with the rest of the traffic, still watching the scene behind him.

CRASH! His cab bumper locked firmly into the rear of a police cruiser ahead. It was more than he could take. Staring wildly, he froze at the wheel.

From far, far away a policeman's voice came to his ears. "Plain case of shock if I ever saw one. Must be new on the job!"

Wilby tugged at the heavy collar, trying to take a back view of the cab crash.

"Sorry, Elwood. You're not going to run away again," Tim's voice was firm.

"Take me home," Wilby demanded, stamping his paw.

"Sure," Tim replied. "But Elwood, first you gotta promise me something."

Wilby, pacing along the hot pavement on all fours, was desperate. "Anything. But get me home."

"First we get back to the truck," Tim explained. "Next we go to Harry's corner. And *next*, you gotta sing, 'Down by the Old Millstream.' "

Wilby's heart sank. "Don't know it," he growled.

"I'll teach you on the way over to Harry's. And remember, Elwood, you've *promised*."

By the time Tim parked at Harry's Corner, Wilby had the song down pat. "Now you just keep going through that routine, Elwood." Tim snapped Elwood's leash to the steering wheel. "You gotta wait here a minute. I gotta go into Harry's first." He leaped out of the truck.

"Put my reading glasses on the dashboard before you do anything," Wilby ordered.

"Okay." Tim reached back into the truck. "But don't you do any reading, Elwood. You just *practice*." He hurried into Harry's.

Wilby folded shaggy paws across his middle and broke into song. "*Down by the old millstream, where I first met you. With your eyes so blue . . .*"

A small dog came trotting past, paused to gaze up into the truck. He stared at Wilby. *Yipe!* Off he went at a dead run down the street.

"Didn't think I was that bad," Wilby muttered. He tuned up again. *"You were sixteen, my village quee-en, down by the old—"*

Out of the corner of his eye he caught a fluttery movement. He looked around. *Elwood was taking shape.*

Wilby glanced at himself. His paws were becoming hands! Elwood's heavy collar was already slipping loosely downward. Wilby removed it and laid it on the seat. "It's a pleasure meeting you—face to face, Elwood. We've been so close these last few days."

He heard hoots of laughter coming from Harry's Corner. Wilby reached for his reading glasses on the dashboard. "Tell Tim that I need these, will you, Elwood?"

He stepped out of the truck. "Well, good luck, ol' buddy." Giving Elwood a friendly pat, he hurried off.

Tim strode out to the truck. "Okay, Elwood. You're on! It's all set. 'Down by the Old Millstream,' then 'The Toreador Song' for an encore. Got it?"

Elwood made no reply.

"Oh, I see you've already snapped off your leash and collar. Good boy! Now come along, Elwood."

Elwood scrambled down off the truck and followed Tim back into Harry's. And for the second time, Elwood failed to live up to advance billing.

Some minutes later, back in the passenger seat, he yawned happily—just as though he hadn't disgraced Tim in front of everybody! Tim looked at

him sadly. "Elwood, I can't help thinking, sometimes. You're really *not* my super-best friend. *Why*
wouldn't you sing? *Why?*"

Elwood looked sad. He snuggled his head on
Tim's lap.

"I know, Elwood," Tim patted him slowly. "You
just weren't in the mood. But it would have meant
so much—to both of us!"

The next day, in the morning sunshine, Betty
and Brian stood, their backs to the interesting
windows of the pawn shop Wilby had just entered.

"Why can't we look in the windows, Mom?"
Brian asked. "There's a lot of good stuff there. I
saw three electric guitars and a lot of other good
stuff just between blinks."

His mother nodded. "Me, too. I spotted a nice
brooch I'd love to have."

"Then why can't we turn around and look?"

"Because we don't want the shop owner to spot
us," Betty answered. "Your father wants to keep
his visit here as private as possible."

"I'll wear a disguise the next time," Brian said
gloomily. "This isn't any fun."

"Just comb your hair and that'll be disguise
enough. Your own mother wouldn't know you."
She eyed Brian a moment. "You haven't mentioned
anything to your friends about—about—"

Brian looked her straight in the eye. "About
Dad? Gosh, Mom. You wouldn't want the kids to
think I'm crazy, would you? Of course I haven't."

Wilby, wearing dark glasses and with his coat

collar turned up, came out the door and joined the family.

"Did you ask how much the brooch cost, Wilby?" Betty asked.

"We're not shopping for a brooch," the D. A. candidate replied. "We're trying to find that ring before I turn into a dog again."

The three moved down the street, Brian walking beside his father. "Dad, if you *do* turn into a dog again, can we go hunting together?"

Wilby almost exploded. "No. We can NOT go hunting together."

Brian lengthened his stride to match Wilby's. "Well, if we can't go hunting together, will you chase Mrs. Metzler's cat?"

Seeing Wilby about to burst into flame, Betty hastily spoke. "Wilby, dear, I hear the ice cream truck bell down the street. Why don't you give Brian some money and let him run on ahead of us?"

"Gladly! Take your time, Brian," his father said. He handed Brian funds for an ice cream sandwich.

As Brian trooped off, Wilby shook his head. "Betty, I'm beginning to wonder about that boy. He seems to be unable to grasp other people's feelings. Asking his own father to chase a cat!"

Betty shook her head. "I think he shows very good sense, Wilby. I mean, when you're *you*, that's okay with Brian. And when you're a dog, that's okay too. He takes things as they are."

"Well, he shouldn't," Wilby replied grumpily. "He ought to be *upset* when I'm a dog."

"Wilby," Betty said gently. "It's *you* who's upset. Brian and I love you anyhow."

Up the street, Brian waited for Tim to make change for another customer, then stepped up. "What flavors you got today, Tim?" he asked.

"Same as always," Tim sighed. "What are you doing in this part of town, Brian?"

"We're looking for a ring with a beetle on it," Brian answered. "What other flavors you got?"

Tim sighed again. Louder. Deeper. "Banana nut, pistachio—. Say, Brian. A ring with a beetle on it? I gave a ring like that to my girl friend. Well, she's not exactly my girl friend yet, but—"

But Brian was off and running. "Dad," he yelled. "Dad!"

It took a bit of time for Wilby to convince Tim that the possible future D. A. should meet Katrinka and ask to see her ring.

It was Elwood who gave Wilby the nod. He licked Wilby's chin in a very welcoming way. That was enough for Tim, but it made Betty uneasy. Never again would Elwood be only the ice cream truck dog to her. "He's *you*, darling," she murmured to Wilby as they drove off to the Dixon plant.

Wilby paled. "Never say that, Betty!" he exclaimed. "He's not me. I'm *him*! Remember that!"

"That's right, Mom," Brian nodded. "It isn't Wilby-Elwood. It's Elwood-Wilby."

Betty pressed a hand to her aching head. "I'll remember, dear. Elwood-Wilby. Elwood-Wilby. I think I have it straight now."

With high hopes, they swirled up to the Dixon loading platform.

8

IT WAS not easy to talk with Katrinka. Wilby found it very hard to discuss a scarab ring with someone who kept right on stacking up pies.

"Please, Miss Muggelberg," he waved his arm toward Tim. "This gentleman unknowingly gave you a ring that really belongs to me. I mean— it doesn't really belong to me, but I need it."

"Tough." Katrinka's rubber-gloved hands never stopped moving.

As Wilby began to plead again, a woman almost Katrinka's size came marching up to the group beginning to gather around. Although her white uniform was exactly the same as the other employees, and her hair just as neatly hidden by the same kind of white cap, anyone could guess she was the boss.

"Just a minute here, sir!" she exclaimed, elbowing her way over to Wilby. "*I* am Head of Pies. If you have any complaints, bring them to me. If it's a personal matter it will have to wait until working hours are over."

"This won't take a moment," said Wilby, not even looking at the Head of Pies. "Miss Muggelberg, I am prepared to offer a reward."

Katrinka brought a strawberry cream pie to a sudden stop mid-air. "How much?"

Brian smiled up at her. "I get a quarter for cleaning the garage. That'll give you an idea. And sometimes I—"

Betty quickly clapped a hand over his mouth and Wilby rushed on while he had the chance to get a word in edgewise. "A thousand dollars," he said, almost choking.

"A thousand dollars! For *that* ring?" Tim gasped.

Every employee in the pie department let fillings and pie crusts fall from their hands. The silence was deadly.

Wilby swallowed. "Okay. Two thousand dollars."

Katrinka whisked flour off her gloves. "Okay. You got yourself a ring, buster."

Slowly she began peeling back a rubber glove. With a blubbery *plop* it pulled free. She stared at her hand. There was no ring.

"Try the other hand," Wilby urged.

No use. On not one of Katrinka's ten powerful fingers was *any* ring.

She forgot about pies, her job, and even the roller derby contest after work. "I *know* I had it," she gasped. "I had it when I started on the lemon meringues."

"Think!" Wilby implored. "*Think!*"

"Think two thousand dollars, Katrinka," Tim begged.

The Head of Pies yanked Wilby around. "If I find it, do I get the reward, mister?"

"I don't care *who* gets the reward," Wilby answered, almost hopping off the floor. "I just want that ring back."

Katrinka frowned. "Now let me see . . . I remember setting it on this shelf right up here when I was asked to make up a special order."

"Which special order?" asked Head of Pies.

"For the hotel," Katrinka answered. "It's already gone out."

There was a sudden dismayed quiet. Then, excepting for Wilby and Betty, every soul in sight bolted out of Dolly Dixon's. Even Brian. "I figure I can use two thousand dollars as well as the next guy," he yelled at his parents over his shoulder.

Led by Head of Pies, the entire department swarmed into the street. Tim grabbed at Katrinka's elbow. "Katrinka, wait! I'll give you a lift in my truck. We'll get there first. Elwood, move over!"

Katrinka almost flung him to the ground. "We go with the Pie Department. What kind of a fink do you think I am?" It was the old Steam Rollers team spirit talking!

Alone on the loading platform, Wilby and Betty watched the pie possé race off for the Medfield-Hilton.

"How about my getting the reward money,

Wilby?" Betty asked, staring after the white clad figures and her only child. "Don't stand there in a daze, Wilby. We shouldn't put *everything* on Brian's shoulders.

As nothing else could have done, the thought of making out a check for two thousand dollars, payable to one Brian Daniels, zipped Wilby into action. "Come on! Into the car!" he yelled.

Away they sped. Behind them a hush fell upon one entire section of Dolly Dixon's Ice Cream and Pies.

Katrinka, Brian, and Head of Pies led the charge into the hotel's kitchen and on to the pantry off the banquet room where all was in readiness for Slade's big night. Cherry pies by the dozens were stacked on every counter space.

An elderly waiter dozing in a chair by the door opened his eyes—and couldn't believe he wasn't still dreaming. White-uniformed figures zoomed from nowhere into everywhere.

He tottered to his feet and snatched the Head of Pies' arm. Too late. Her hands seized upon an innocent pie doing no harm to anyone. In seconds, it was permanently wounded. Cherries and crust flying in all directions! No ring!

"Madame!" the waiter cried out. "Stop that! Stop, I say." He tried in vain to snatch at her wrist.

Without mercy, she slammed the bottom crust square in his face. Instantly, the waiter forgot the welfare of the pies. Revenge was sweet—and a cherry pie revenge even sweeter. *Smack*. Head of

Pies dodged—and Katrinka caught it between the eyes!

"Nobody does that to *my* girl and gets away with it!" Tim yelled, seeing red all over but especially on his darling. He caught up a pie. It was a blind pitch. Though it missed the mark, it did catch the splendidly dressed *maître d'*, head of the banquet room, as he came through the swinging doors. *Slam!*

But he had not risen to his high position by not keeping his wits about him. Before the first drop of cherry juice splattered off his shirt front, he shouted out commands. "Help! All waiters to pantry! Help!" he roared.

At his cry, the same fighting spirit that made Katrinka the number one Steam Roller went firing along every line of her powerful frame. She snatched Tim off his feet. "My hero!" she cried, giving him a cherry-flavored kiss and two cracked ribs.

Blue-jacketed waiters streamed in to aid their fallen leader. Cherry pies, blue jackets, white uniforms! Foot for foot, the pantry had the most patriotic look of any room in the United States— up to and including Hawaii and Alaska.

"At 'em girls!" screeched Katrinka, dropping Tim like a wet flag and giving another pie an illegal spitball pitch.

Out in the lobby, Wilby and Betty came whirling through the revolving doors. "Look, Wilby!" Betty pointed to the bulletin board. "John Slade's cherry pie festival!" She paled. "Oh, Wilby! The pies must have been for this auction. *It's already begun, and our team is still looking for the ring!*

Those pies aren't going to stand a chance!"

"We'd better go out and come in again by the back door," Wilby said, clutching her elbow. "Hurry!"

But speed was impossible. Between the bulletin board and the revolving doors, the lobby had suddenly become a mass of parading John Slade supporters. Two by two, girls and young men in costume and all wearing stiff-brim straw hats came stepping high in a figure-eight pattern. Every voice was raised in song. To the strains of "When Johnny Comes Marching Home Again," they loudly hooted out:

> Honest John's the man for us,
> D. A., D. A.!
> And we're not afraid
> It won't be Slade
> Hurray! Hurray!
> How the girls will laugh and
> The boys will shout
> When Wilby Daniels
> Fades right out—

There was more, but Wilby had his mind on fading out of the lobby. "Sounds worse than the Daisy Hymn," he said grimly. "But what a turnout!"

"Forget the turnout, Wilby. How do we get to the pies? Take it from your campaign manager, Slade is going to holler, 'dirty politics!' "

That was enough for Wilby. Cutting through the lower half of the figure eight, the Danielses made what was almost a flying tackle on the revolving doors.

Going at top speed, they reached the banquet room pantry just in time to see Brian use the famous Brian Daniels Frisby Curve on a deluxe model pie.

In the banquet room, the auctioneer was holding up one of the few pies that was to survive the historic Cherry Pie Massacre.

"Two hundred. Sold! Thanks, Jim. Remember, folks, all proceeds go into the Honest John Slade War Chest—so let's give big for Honest John!"

Raymond edged up to his boss. "It's going very well, isn't it?"

Honest John nodded. "Even better than last year." He glanced back toward the pantry and frowned a bit. "It seems a little noisy in there."

In the pantry, Wilby grabbed his son. "Brian! Cut it *out*! We'll never find that ring!" He turned to the entire battlefield. "Folks! Please! *Please*! We'll never find—"

His speech was cut short by pie in the eye, hurled by Head of Pies.

Blood, as well as cherries, rushed to Wilby's head. Before Head of Pies could blink, Wilby lobbed one back. It missed target and went sailing through a window.

Outside the hotel, Dip, strolling past with Freddie, caught the flying missile. The sight of his partner mopping up cherries sent Freddie into gulping fits of joy. But not for long! *POW*! Freddie caught a pie on the ear. It was Dip's turn to double over.

Half-furious, half-drowning in pie crust, Freddie

mopped at his splattered self. Something scratched along his jaw. "Hey, Dip! Look at this!" He held out his handkerchief. "It's that *ring!*"

"How'd it get into a cherry pie?" Dip gasped.

"Why ask?" Freddie shrugged. "I sold it once, I'll sell it again."

Inside the pantry, noise had reached such a pitch that Honest John decided to put a stop to it.

"Come on, Raymond. Sometimes these people forget their positions."

"But they're voters, boss," Raymond reminded him.

"Forget it!" Honest John flicked his cigar and pushed against the swinging door to the pantry, his face set in stern "cut-it-out" lines.

Alas for Honest John's stern lines. Pies hit the two men, each dead center. In an instant, Slade and Raymond were covered with cherries and broken crust. Only a still-smoking cigar survived the attack.

Wilby froze. His next-to-worst dream was coming true! "I'm terribly sorry, Mr. Slade," he gulped, trying to locate Honest John's eyes. "We were just looking for a ring and—and things got out of hand."

Slade peered through the pie blobs. "Daniels, I've run a clean race *so* far. But this is *too* much." Picking up one of the few remaining pies, he pushed it flat into Wilby's worried face.

Betty charged forward. "Why you—you—you *pompous*—" Words failed her. She heaved a pie at Slade. It missed. But Brian curved one *splat* across the back of Honest John's head.

"Brian!" Wilby shouted through a red haze.

"I know, Dad. Don't bother. I know— 'Brian, cut it out!' "

It was hard to believe, but finally everybody, including Dip and Freddie, were once more neatly cleaned up. "There's still time, Freddie. Why don't you hit the street and make our dinner money?"

Freddie stretched. "Okay, Dip. Gimme the ring."

Luck was with him not two blocks down the street. He spotted a parked car, and behind the wheel sat a bored-looking driver. Freddie stepped up. "Pardon me, sir. But may I introduce myself?"

The man listened carefully as Freddie ran through his sad story of why he had to part with a valuable ring.

"I wonder if you might be interested?" asked Freddie, winding up his sales talk.

"I sure would be," said the stranger. He reached into his pocket and flipped out his police badge. "Get in, buddy. A lot of folks are interested."

Dinner at the Daniels house was timed for the evening TV news. The first local news item made Wilby Daniels drop his knife and fork. "The Prescott Museum's priceless ring has been recovered!" Wilby repeated the newscaster's words like a parrot.

In seconds, the diners had fled the table, were out the door, and into the driveway. Minutes later, they pulled up in front of the police station.

Wilby was first out of the car. He whizzed up

the station steps, Betty and Brian bolting after him.

Breathlessly, he spoke to the desk sergeant. "We understand that the Prescott Museum ring has been recovered."

The sergeant eyed him coldly. "Whadda you got to do with it?"

"Ah—er—it's personal," Wilby replied.

"The lieutenant will be out in a minute. They're making the identification out in the back room now."

Wilby turned pale. *"And reading the inscription. Sergeant, let me go back there. That's just it. I can't take a chance!"*

Eyes cold as glass, the desk sergeant stared at Wilby. "Wait over there," he said sternly.

In the back room of the station, a police lieutenant could hardly keep Professor Whatley from dancing with joy. "Be calm, Professor," he said soothingly. "Everything is under control. You've got the ring and we've got the thief." He guided the professor out to the front desk.

Wilby looked up as they entered. The professor was still talking one-to-the-dozen. "I'm relieved just to have it out of circulation," he said. "It's supposed to have supernatural powers, you know. Notice the inscription here—*In Canis Corpore Transmuto*."

Wilby's hand flew to his face. "I knew it. I knew it," he muttered.

Brian looked over at his father. "Oh, gosh!" he breathed. He leaned over to Betty who was eyeing the arrival of Honest John Slade's assistant, Raymond. "Mom!" he whispered. "There goes Pop again."

Betty sprang to her feet. "Oh, Wilby," she moaned. "No!"

Luckily the lieutenant was so interested in the ring that he didn't notice the callers sitting on the bench. "What does that mean, Professor—that *In Canis* stuff?"

"It's like a command, Lieutenant. It's in Latin, of course. It means, 'into a dog's body change.' "

Betty and Brian stood up, Wilby at their feet.

"Heel, boy!" Betty commanded, and began walking to the street door.

"Good evening, Mrs. Daniels," Raymond said politely. "May I open the door for you?" He glanced down at Wilby.

"Thank you," Betty replied in a chilly voice. The door swung shut behind them.

"Aren't you gonna ask about the ring, Dad?" Brian looked down at the shaggy dog trotting beside him.

"I'll come back," Wilby answered his son. "But not until I'm *more myself*."

Raymond, on the other side of the door, looked around. Candidate Daniels was not in sight. "That's funny," he muttered. "What were his wife and kid doing here?" He shrugged. "Probably out getting information for him. Lot of good it will do Daniels. Under Honest John Slade, the D. A.'s office will break this case!"

His attention was caught by Professor Whatley. He listened. "The late Dr. Plumcott of the Prescott Museum told me several years ago of an incident where a young man—a teenager—I believe, was actually transformed into a dog, due to the strange powers of the ring."

The lieutenant smiled. "But you don't believe that, do you, Professor?"

Professor Whatley half-laughed, half-frowned. "Well, not really. Still, I'm careful. I don't like to repeat those words too often. I might become sensitized. You know—turn into a dog myself."

Both the professor and the lieutenant chuckled over that—but not Raymond. *A dog. A shaggy dog*! Like the last piece of a jigsaw puzzle, Raymond picked up those words and dropped them neatly into place.

Turning on his heel, he rushed out. "Here's where I get a raise!" he muttered gleefully. "Is Honest John ever going to thank me for this one!"

9

"SO WILBY DANIELS is a dog?" Honest John Slade leaned back in his desk chair and eyed Raymond closely. He chomped down on his cigar. "I hate to tell you this, Raymond, but you've lost your marbles."

"Lost my marbles!" Raymond exclaimed. "Mr. Slade, you haven't understood a word I've been saying. Sometimes Daniels is a *real* dog. I haven't lost my marbles. I've found the taw. Shoot it and the game's yours!"

Interest flickered in John Slade's eyes. He hadn't forgotten those days when a taw could be the winner for the kid who used it right. "Yeah? Tell me more."

"Remember Daniels' TV show? Remember that dog?" Raymond asked eagerly. *"That dog was*

Daniels. And it's happened twice since. At the Daisies' meeting Daniels disappeared into thin air and that same shaggy dog came tearing out into the lobby. I was there. I saw it. Then the same thing happened not an hour ago at the police station. I saw that dog again with Mrs. Daniels and the kid—but no Daniels. *And this ring does it*." He held it out. "I got it from the lieutenant at the station. I—er—took the liberty of using your name to get it."

Slade took the ring and stared at it. He rubbed his eyes. Glow, fade, fade, glow. He pushed it back across the desk blotter.

"Please, Mr. Slade," Raymond begged. "Get Daniels over here. You'll find out for yourself."

"Thought you said he was a dog, Raymond. I'm not running for dog-catcher, you know."

Raymond wriggled. "Well, maybe he's changed back by now. Please, Mr. Slade."

A look of pity came into Slade's eyes. "Now take it easy, Raymond. You've been working too hard on my campaign, boy."

"Please!"

Honest John stood up. "Tell you what I'll do. You get a good night's sleep. Then if you still feel the same way tomorrow—well, *maybe* I'll call him."

Raymond bit his lip. "Perhaps you're right, Mr. Slade. It'll give Daniels a chance to change back from being a dog. That'd make it easier for you to talk with him, I guess. But I could tell you right now what you're supposed to do when you show him the ring, Mr. Slade."

Slade patted his assistant's shoulder. "Tomorrow.

Tomorrow, Raymond. Plenty of time. Now you turn in. We'll all feel better in the morning. This has been a terrible day. Terrible. I'll never order cherry pie the rest of my life!"

Honest John didn't have to ask Wilby to appear in his office. Wilby, planning all along to call on the D. A. and explain that dirty politics was the last thing he had in mind during the cherry pie festival, appeared in the late afternoon.

Overnight Slade had given some more thought to what Raymond had told him. "Maybe," Slade was thinking by the time Wilby entered his office, "the ring bit works."

An evil smile on his lips, Slade listened to Wilby's explanation. "Hmm." He leaned back in his chair. "That's all very interesting, Daniels. But I'm going to make you a deal. I want you to drop out of the race. Give any reason you want."

Wilby sprang to his feet. "No way. And you listen to me, Mr. District Attorney! I don't make deals. I can live down the cherry pie fight. And I'm in the race right to the finish." He leaned his fists on Slade's desk. "I'm going to get elected, and my first duty will be to call a grand jury investigation into your criminal connections in this city." He straightened up and glared across at Slade. "So if that's all we have to talk about, this discussion is closed."

Slade only smiled. "That's up to you, of course. Oh, by the way, is this the ring you were looking for in my pie auction?"

Wilby stared. It certainly was. He tried to keep

his voice cool and steady. "Yes, that does look like it." He moved forward, holding out his hand. "Thank you so much, Mr. Slade."

Slade pulled the ring back out of reach. "You're *sure*, Daniels? There's an inscription in here." He held up the ring. " '*In Canis Corpore Transmuto*,' " he read. "That sound familiar?" He repeated it.

"Give me that!" Wilby demanded, and stuck out—a *paw*.

Slade flipped a lever on his desk intercom. "Raymond? Will you come in, please?"

As Raymond entered, his eyes fastened on a very large, shaggy dog. He beamed joyously.

"Raymond, this dog has no license and is in violation of the leash law. Inform the dog pound, please."

"I've already taken the liberty to do so," Raymond smirked. "They're waiting outside the building."

Beneath his fringe of shaggy curls, Wilby's eyes glinted dangerously. "Pipsqueak!" he said distinctly. He took a quick look around. Foolishly, Raymond had not closed the door after he had come into the office. Wilby bolted, pausing on his way only long enough to hook Raymond with a powerful left.

"Grab him!" the D. A. yelled.

No use. Raymond was not in shape to grab a falling snowflake. Out Wilby went. Looking neither left nor right, he zoomed straight on, up and over Slade's secretary's desk. For the briefest moment, he sat on her lap. "Excuse me!" he breathed, and raced off to the hall door in time to knock down a staff member carrying a big stack of campaign leaflets. The leaflets sailed into the air and fell in a white blizzard. Slade came crashing through it, followed by his dazed assistant.

"I've never seen such a bunch of nincompoops in my life," Slade yelled, heading for the hallway. "After him!"

Wilby skidded toward an open window at the end of the hall. Outside, two painters worked from a hanging scaffold high above the ground. It was a tough decision, but Wilby made it fearlessly.

With Slade's entire office staff pounding behind him, out the window and down the rope Wilby went. High above his head, Slade leaned out the window, shouting to the men in the pound truck, "Follow that dog!" and shouting to Raymond, "You, too! Down that rope! Get that dog! GO ON!"

Wilby landed on the sidewalk but couldn't stop long enough to lick the rope burns on his smarting paws. One look at the pound truck, and he took off like a heavy cannonball.

Howie and Sheldon, the men in the truck, didn't wait for Raymond's arrival. They went speeding off down the street and made a hard right as Wilby turned into an alley. Raymond, on foot, came panting after them. No shaggy dog was in sight— naturally, as Wilby had safely tucked himself into a garbage can.

Unluckily, he came peeping out a bit too soon. The can lid crashed noisily to the pavement. Sheldon, the driver, put the truck in reverse and shot backwards. Raymond dodged out of its path, as did Wilby. In a flash, he was off, heading for a pleasant green park not far away.

"Rest! I have to have rest!" he panted. He looked around at the park benches. Plenty of people were resting. In fact, they were asleep.

Quickly, Wilby helped himself to one sleeper's hat and another's newspaper. Not until the dog pound truck whizzed past, did Wilby return the borrowed property. "Thanks," he murmured to the sleeper, and trotted off.

"If I know Slade, he's going to have the police after me," Wilby muttered. "I'd better not head for home just yet." He looked down to check his hands. Alas! They were still paws. He shrugged. "Well, there's nothing to do but make the best of it. And if it comes to running, four feet will be better than two. I'll just sort of ease along after it's dark. Maybe Admiral Brenner's flowering shrub would be the best possible place for the night. At least there, I'd be right next door to Betty and Brian."

Wilby had sized up Slade's actions just about right. The D. A. was on the phone to the Chief of Police.

"Chief, there's a mad dog on the loose in this city, and those fools from the pound don't seem able to catch him. I need your assistance . . . every car that's available." He followed that up with a brief description. "Thanks, Chief! Do as much for you someday!"

His office door opened. A pale, weary Raymond stepped in. He headed for a large leather chair and dropped into it.

"Get up!" Slade snapped. "Order my limousine. We're joining the police in a street-by-street search."

Raymond staggered to his aching feet and lurched out of the office. "Why did I ever go into politics?" he moaned.

In the back seat of the D. A.'s limousine, he had a chance to rest his frame. But after an hour of cruising Medfield, he turned to Slade. "Why can't we just make a public announcement saying that sometimes Daniels is a dog?"

Slade snorted. "You know who they'd put away first, don't you? Us."

The car telephone rang. Slade grabbed it. "Slade here."

Howie, in the pound truck, spoke into his radio mike. "Mr. Slade, the suspect has been seen heading west on Crescent. They got a tail on him."

"Close in!" Slade shouted. "Surround him."

Everyone in that part of Medfield was sure a dangerous criminal was about to be cornered. Sirens wailed from all directions. Traffic moved over to let police cruisers zoom through. Even Wilby, at first, could not imagine that this wild show of law and order was in his honor. But as he crossed an intersection kitty-corner style, he spotted the pound truck and three police cruisers racing toward him from the four streets. "I'm in big trouble," he groaned. At the top of his racing form, he shot away between the nearest cars.

Behind him came the sound of an enormous crash. He glanced back. Three cruisers and a truck—a beautiful four-way fender bender! Usually a kindly sort, Wilby smiled in satisfaction. He looked about and a large lighted sign caught his eye.

ROLLERDROME
JERSEY JUGGERNAUTS
VS.
THE STEAM ROLLERS

"Now where have I heard that name before?" Willy frowned, staring up. "Oh, yes. Miss Muggelberg, of course."

A cry sounded almost on top of his left ear. "Elwood! Where on earth have you been?"

Wilby's heart sank. "I might have known it! Where there's a Katrinka, there'll be a Tim. If he grabs me, I'm sunk!" He gathered his strength and pushed out breathlessly, charging past Tim, the Rollerdrome ticket taker, and all others in his path. In moments, he was flashing past Miss Muggelberg, herself, as she whizzed along the oval track followed by madly careening skaters.

Horror filled Wilby's eyes. "I'm almost on the track! Everybody will see me!"

Even worse, Slade's voice rang out from only a short distance away. "Let me through! I'm the district attorney. Official business!"

Wilby beat it—straight down a passageway leading away from the banked oval of the track. Where to hide? He had no choice—through the door marked

STEAM ROLLERS DRESSING ROOM
LADIES ONLY

But old habits die hard. He knocked first. "Anybody inside?" he called. No answer. In he went.

Outside, led by Slade, Elwood, dog pounders, and police rushed up and down aisles, to the boos of paying customers who had come to see Katrinka, not the D. A.

Over the P. A. system the announcer's voice brimmed with excitement. "There's the bell signaling for a jam," he cried. "We'll see some action now as Captain Katrinka Muggelberg tries to get a teammate through the Juggernaut jam."

Tim stopped in his tracks to view Katrinka's great moment. Raymond kept his mind on his work. "Nothing on our side," he screamed. And Slade yelled back, "Search the dressing rooms."

As the Steam Rollers' dressing room door flung in, Wilby, in full Steam Roller uniform, skated out. Slade's mouth dropped open as Wilby coasted off toward the track. "After him!" he bawled.

Wilby reached the track guard rail, ducked under, and at top speed caught up with the other skaters.

"Pretty smart dog!" Howie gasped. "Look at him go!"

"Stop yammering! Go in there and get him!" Slade pushed Howie to the rail.

"Yes, sir." Net in hand, Howie started timidly over the rail.

From the P. A. system, a puzzled announcer called out, "The Steam Rollers have fielded a new skater. I'm not quite certain who she is."

"*She*! I've got 'em fooled!" Wilby's spirits lifted and he rounded a curve even faster.

But even though he could hardly believe his eyes, Tim wasn't fooled. *Elwood was trying to pass Katrinka!* He shuddered. He loved them both!

Katrinka's hand shot out and seized Wilby. With one powerful motion, she slung Wilby out front, then almost reeled when she caught sight of the shaggy hair in her fingers. "That was no hand I grabbed. It was a *paw!*"

But a small thing like losing a handful of hair meant nothing to Wilby. Not only had Katrinka flung him right through the Juggernaut defense, she had boosted him all the way to the guard rail.

Wilby jumped, swept along an aisle between customers, and went sailing out the Rollerdrome door—straight up to Tim's ice cream truck. Quickly he hopped in the driver's seat.

Chasing after his dear friend, Tim managed to board the truck from the end platform just as it pulled away.

He crawled up to the wire mesh that separated the Dolly Dixon supplies from the driver's section. "Elwood! You were wonderful! Why didn't you tell me you could skate? That'll be a real show-stopper! Listen, Elwood. How about this? Tim and his Amazing Dog, Elwood. He talks, he sings, he skates, he . . . *drives*? Elwood! *Take your foot, uh paw, off the gas pedal!* You'll get in trouble."

"I'm in trouble already. Big trouble," Wilby answered, driving faster.

"What'd you *do*, Elwood?"

Wilby glanced into the rearview mirror. A parade of headlights was gaining on the ice cream truck. "Tell you later, Tim. Start throwing out that stuff in the back. Everything. Pies, ice cream, syrup—all you got."

Tim's voice shook with shock. "They cost me money, Elwood."

"Throw it out!" Wilby yelled. "I told you we'd talk later."

Talk later! Tim's eyes suddenly glowed. Once more he could see a signed contract with Elwood's paw on the dotted line. He shot to the back of the truck. *Wham! Slam! Plop! Bloop!* Hardly an inch of bare pavement showed below a carpet of slippery Dolly Dixon dainties.

"Elwood! Y'oughta see them skid!" he yelled.

"Still coming?" Wilby glanced back.

It was only a split-second look away from the street ahead. But a split second was all it took.

"Look out!" Tim roared—almost as well as Admiral Brenner would have done it.

Too late! Wilby tried hard to swing around the street repair barricade just ahead. No use! The ice cream truck came to a jarring halt on a mound of rocks and dirt.

Wilby leaped from the truck. "Sorry, Tim. We will talk later. But right now I've got a better chance *on paw.*"

In a burst of speed, his shaggy form headed into a wooded area—Medfield's Genevieve E. Slade Park.

Slade's limousine whirled up and stopped at the curb. Honest John took one look at the dark, winding paths beneath the big trees, and cursed the day his grandmother gave the land to the city. If she'd taken his advice, she'd have sold it to the nearest lumber mill and Wilby Daniels would be in plain sight this very minute.

He stepped out of the limousine, Raymond following. "Did the professor say how long this spell would last?" he asked furiously.

"I didn't ask him," Raymond answered.

"You wouldn't," Slade snapped. He grabbed the ring from his pocket. "Well, I'm not taking any chances. *In Canis Corpore Transmuto.*"

Raymond reached for the ring. "I'll do that for you, sir," he said humbly.

"I can cast my own spells, thanks. *In Canis Corpore Transmuto.*"

From the limousine came the ring of the telephone. Slade bumped Raymond out of the way to grab it first. "Slade here."

Howie came on, excitement in his voice. "We got him surrounded, sir. In Vista Grove."

"Hold him 'til I get there." Slade slammed down the phone. "Jump in, Raymond. We're on our way!"

10

"THIS IS the end," Wilby panted, looking down from his perch in the crotch of a large oak. Slade's limousine was pulling into the ring of headlights shining on the tree. "The wagons have circled," Wilby moaned, "only this time the Indian's in the middle."

A fresh look of alarm sprang into his weary eyes as he spotted Howie lifting a rifle. "My gosh! Is there *nothing* Slade won't stop at!"

To his relief, it wasn't to be murder. Slade yelled out, "Be ready with that tranquilizing gun."

"Just say the word!" replied Howie, taking aim.

Slade strode up and climbed onto a park bench at the foot of the oak. "Daniels," he said in a low voice, "I'll give you one last chance. Withdraw from the race—or else."

"I'm in this race to the end, Slade," Wilby replied firmly.

Of all the deputy dog-hunters present, only Howie was close enough to see and almost hear the conversation taking place between Medfield's powerful district attorney and the shaggy mutt in the tree. In all his dog-catching experience, he had never before captured a talking tree-climber. Furthermore, up until now, he'd thought that D. A.s did their talking in courtrooms. *Talking?* He lowered the rifle and mopped his forehead with his sleeve. "I'm going crazy," he muttered.

Over by the cars a policeman called out, "Don't try to coax him down, Mr. Slade. Remember, that's a mad dog up there."

Slade paid no attention to the warning. "So you're in the race to the end, are you? You sure are, Daniels. The end's right now!"

He climbed down from the bench and shouted to Howie, "Shoot him down!"

But Howie could not control his trembling hands. He fumbled with the trigger. "It won't work, sir," he called over to Slade.

Howie's partner, Sheldon, came running up to help. "I think you have to release a safety trigger first, Howie. Here. Let me look."

As he touched the trigger, there was a sudden sharp report. *Zip!* Faster than the eye could see, a dart pierced the air and went on to pierce District Attorney Honest John Slade's rump.

"OUCH!" Slade's hand went slamming down on the sting.

Howie rushed up. "Very sorry, sir. It was accidental. Really it was. Could I make up for it by giving you my vote on Election Day?" he asked worriedly.

"You numbskull!" Slade roared. "Don't you know how to do *anything* right? Load up that thing again and—"

His words trailed off. He slid to the ground, eyes closed.

Howie looked down at him. "Okay!" he said coldly. "So I won't give you my vote. *I'm* no numbskull."

Up in the tree, Wilby's shaggy sides heaved with mirth.

Alas! Not for long! *Zip* went another dart.

And he wasn't laughing at all when he woke up. Bars of shadow fell across his shaggy coat. He squinted groggily. "I must be in jail," he muttered. He lifted his aching head and looked around. Horror swept him from nose to tail. "Jail!" he exclaimed. "I'm in the *dog pound!*"

Feebly he staggered to his shaggy paws. A jaunty looking black and white terrier trotted over. "Whaddaya in for, sweetheart?"

Wilby stared. *He'd* never met a talking dog before!

"Come on. Meet the gang. I'm Bogie. That's Jimmy over there, and Eddie and Peter. Up there in her own private cell—that's Mae."

Wilby's cellmates and Mae each greeted the newcomer. "This your first rap, Curly?" Mae called down.

Dazed, Wilby managed to answer, "Yeah."

"Welcome to one-way row, pal," Bogie said.

"One-way row?" Wilby repeated. "Say, what's 'one-way row,' exactly?"

"It ain't Westminster Kennel," Mae answered gloomily.

Peter, a dignified, too thin but still handsome setter, shook his head. "Curly my boy, it's the slammer. And I mean the slammer. Three days in—then out. And I do mean *out*!"

Wilby stared, horrified. "I got to get out of here," he cried.

"Don't we all?" Eddie shrugged. "Not a hope, pal."

Wilby looked around desperately. Bars and steel mesh everywhere! His glance went to an iron drainage grate on the floor. His eyes glinted. "I don't go for that 'not a hope' stuff," he said. "Where there's a will, there's a way. And where there's an iron grate, there's *something* underneath it. Come on, fellows! I got an idea."

In the police station, the sergeant unlocked Tim's handcuffs. "He's all yours, lady," he said to Katrinka.

She counted the change left after paying Tim's bail. "Yeah," she said shortly. "Come on, Tim."

"Katrinka, it wasn't my fault," Tim began, even before they were out the station door. "Elwood was driving and—"

"*That's* what you're going to tell a judge?"

"Well, I don't want to get Elwood in trouble, of course, but he was driving and—"

"And then he jumped over the moon. Right? Come on. Let's get out of here. You need fresh air." She jerked him down the station steps.

Hurrying to keep up with Katrinka's stride, Tim tried to explain his story. "Katrinka, you could at least *listen*. You're being unreasonable."

Katrinka threw up her hands. "*Me* unreasonable!"

"Don't worry about the bail money, Katrinka. I'm soon going to be rolling in money." He lowered his voice. "I wasn't going to tell you this, Katrinka, because I wanted to surprise you. But Elwood and me are putting an act together." He leaned close to her ear. "Now get this—Tim and his Talking Dog."

"His *talking* dog?"

"Yes, talking. Elwood can talk. We're trying to work out the details of the contract. Elwood's playing a little hard to get right now, but he'll be showing up. You can count on that."

He held up his fingers. "I might go four million for Elwood and one for me. But that is absolute tops. I've got to find that dog and get this contract business straightened out."

Katrinka stopped walking. She stared. Tim marched right on, still talking and counting on his fingers.

She shook her head—almost sadly.

"Brian," Betty Daniels said, "will you please turn down the TV? I have to make a telephone call."

Brian not only turned down the volume, but turned off the set. As his mother opened the phone book, he stared out the window and began whistling, "Oh Where, O Where has my Little Dog Gone?"

"Brian, will you stop whistling that? After all, this is nothing to sing about."

"I wasn't singing about. I was whistling about," Brian replied, turning around. "Who're you going to call, Mom?"

Betty pretended not to hear. Most boys' mothers would not be thinking of calling the city dog pound for a missing husband. She dialed the number. Howie answered.

"Ah, yes, uh—" Betty began, hesitating. "This is—er, a dog owner. I seem to have lost my dog, and I was wondering if by any chance you might have him. I'm afraid he wasn't wearing his license when he left the house."

"Can you describe the animal, Ma'am?" Howie asked.

"Oh, yes. He's tall, nice hair, charming disposition. And he's quite handsome, *I* think. He has soft brown eyes and—what did you say?"

"I said it sounds more like you're looking for Rock Hudson. Just gimme the breed and color and we'll start from there."

"Oh. Just a minute, please." She put her hand over the receiver. "Brian, what breed would you say your father was?"

"Sheepdog. Are you calling the pound, Mom?"

"Ssh!" She turned back to the phone. "Sheepdog. More gray than white, I'd say."

"Mmm. Well, we did get a long-haired dog in. But this one is a real killer."

"That doesn't sound like my husband. Thank

you." She hung up, leaving Howie staring, shocked, at his phone. "*Husband*. Did she say husband?"

For once, Brian didn't say anything Brian-like. Instead, he patted Betty's shoulder. "Don't worry, Mom. Pop can take care of himself."

On a sofa in the Slade living room, Honest John stretched out flat on his stomach while Raymond placed a soothing ice bag on his employer's wound.

"Don't worry, Mr. Slade. I saw them cart him away, myself. In seventy-two hours, he'll be a goner."

"Seventy-two *hours*. Raymond, get on that phone and get me the governor. I'm not going to take any chances. I'm not waiting any seventy-two hours!"

It was Wilby who managed to lift the iron grate. Then Jimmy and Bogie, being smallest, were first to start the digging of a tunnel leading off from the drain space. Dirt and rocks flew. Otherwise, there was a strange, tense quiet in the slammer.

"Hurry up, pal," Bogie whispered to his teammate. "We don't have all night."

"I'm digging. I'm digging," Jimmy panted.

"Wish I was going with you," Mae said sadly from her separate cell.

"Don't worry, Mae," Pete spoke gloomily. "Nobody's going to get out of here. We're never going to make it. They'll get us all."

Bogie looked around. "We're bustin' outta here. You with us, or not?"

Peter glanced over to where Wilby was keeping

watch on the office door, down the hall. "He could be a stoolie."

Wilby left the bars and trotted briskly over to the tunnel opening. "I assure you, I am no stoolie. I'm not even a dog. My name is Wilby Daniels, and I'm running for district attorney of Medfield."

There was a sharp silence. The others traded glances. Then Jimmy, shaking the tunnel dust from his sides, eyed Wilby coldly. "Will you listen to this palooka? Why I ought to mop the floor with you!"

From down the hall came the sound of a door opening and closing. Then came footsteps and the jingling of keys.

"Whadda I tell you?" Peter asked.

Quickly, Jimmy and Bogie shoved the iron grate back into place. "That's the breaks, pals," Bogie sighed. "Another two minutes and we'da made it."

"Curly was settin' us up for this," Pete said angrily. "Didn't see *him* diggin'. Did'ja?"

Howie stepped into the big cell. He went past all but Wilby. Quietly, he led him out, locking the kennel cell behind him. At the end of the hallway, he bent down. "Sorry, boy," he said, patting Wilby on the head. "Governor's orders."

"Governor's orders!" Wilby gasped. Every muscle tightened. "Not this dog, you don't!"

With a wild leap he bunted Howie to the floor. "Sit!" Wilby commanded, turning the tables on the astounded deputy dog catcher.

Howie made a slight move. "Stay!" Wilby roared.

Quickly, Wilby snatched Howie's keys. He galloped back and unlocked the cell door. "Let's go, boys. Start digging. I've got to spring Mae."

While the others leaped to the job, Wilby sorted out keys. In moments, Mae was free to join the group. "You're a real blue-ribbon sport, Curly," she choked. "I'll never forget this."

Jimmy's muffled voice sounded from the tunnel. "I'm almost through."

"Make it fly, pal," called Bogie.

Once again there was only the sound of digging. Then Jimmy's voice called out the good news. "Okay! I made it! All you mugs under the wall. Quick!"

Wilby, their new leader, was invited to go first. "Thanks, but I'm biggest. I don't want to get stuck and spoil this caper. But on your way out, pick up a little dirt if you can. Then maybe I can make it."

"Will we ever!" Mae breathed. "Curly, for you— anything!"

As Wilby was making his exit into the night air, Sheldon, the pound driver, was parking the dog-catcher truck at the pound entrance. He entered the building, carrying a late-evening snack for himself and Howie. He looked around. No Howie. "That's funny!" he muttered.

It was another minute or two before he saw the door to the kennel cells was ajar. He strode toward it, calling out, "Howie! I got us fresh dough-nuts and coffee, and the coffee's getting cold. You'd better— *Howie*! What are you doing on the floor?"

"That big dog told me to sit here."

Sheldon stared. "You probably just need a vacation, Howie. Come on. We'll take a look. I'm sure that dog is right back there where he belongs. He *couldn't* have been out here."

Together, they went back to the main cell. Not a dog was in sight. Even Mae was gone!

Outside, the others waited for Wilby. No sooner did he come panting out than he spotted Sheldon's truck. "There's our getaway car. Pile in."

"I don't drive," said Bogie.

"I do," Wilby replied sharply. "Hurry."

Mae jumped in first. "I'd follow you anywhere, Curly." She looked at him, thankfulness beaming in her eyes.

Last aboard was dignified Peter. He made it just in time. Wilby swirled out from the curb, as Sheldon, net in hand, came racing out the front door, Howie tottering behind him. Stunned, they saw the inmates zoom off.

Inside, the telephone rang. Howie muttered weakly, "I'll get it." He hurried back.

Shakily, he picked up the receiver. "Howie here. Oh, Mr. Slade. Yes."

Slade held the ice bag in one hand and the phone in the other. "I'm just calling to confirm that you've carried out the governor's orders."

"Well . . . uh—"

" 'Uh' what, man? Did you or didn't you?"

"We've had a little problem here, sir. There's been a breakout."

"A *breakout!*"

"Yes, sir. All the dogs drove off in our truck."

"You dummy!" came through the receiver so loudly that Howie jumped in the air and landed solidly on his backside.

Wilby's passengers went rocking along in a state of joy, but Wilby was silent behind the wheel.

Bogie glanced at him. "What's the matter, sweetheart? You look a little down in the dumps."

Wilby frowned. "Look. We'd better ditch the truck and split up."

"Okay on ditching," Mae agreed. "But why split up, Curly? Why not run with us, handsome?"

"Thanks, Mae, but I've got a problem. There's a ring I need.

"Yeah?" Jimmy asked. "What kinda ring?"

"Well, it's old and it has—oh, never mind, fellas." He brought the truck to a stop and leaped out. "You got a better chance without me. So long!"

"Thanks, Curly. We won't forget what you done for us, see?" Eddie nodded sadly.

"Tail up, pal," Jimmy added. "Just remember— somewhere there's a backyard with your name on it!"

As Wilby trotted off into the night, his new friends looked worried. "Say, guys," Bogie shook his head, "there's a kid that's really got a problem."

Eddie waggled an ear. "He gave us a lift. We give him a lift. Sooner or later we'll be running into him again. Know what I mean?"

All nodded agreement.

Sticking with his first idea, Wilby settled down

behind Admiral Brenner's flowering shrub. And none too soon! The beam of a searchlight on a passing cruiser flung a long light across the lawn.

After it was far down the block, Wilby arose and plunked his large shaggy paws down the length of the Admiral's flower bed. He hurried toward his own house, while back in The Flagship, the Admiral grabbed the telephone to call the police.

"It's that same woolly mammoth, I tell you. What difference does it make what color it is? It's him, all right. On the double now, sergeant. That's what I pay taxes for. I'll expect you *immediately*!"

Wilby reached the side of his house and went to a lighted window. He batted a paw against the pane.

"Look, Mom!" Brian yelled. "It's Pop!"

Betty pushed open the window. "Oh, darling. We've been so worried. What's happening?"

Together, she and Brian helped Wilby to heave his shaggy bulk over the sill.

"Pull the drapes, Betty," he panted.

"We don't have any, dear. Calm down."

"Calm *down*? Betty, Slade's got the ring, and unless I can get it back, he's going to rub me out."

"Wilby! NO!" Betty cried.

Police sirens wailed in the distance. Betty cried out again. "Wilby! YES. Hide!"

"Can't, honey. I've got to get out of here."

"What're you going to do?" she asked fearfully.

"Nail Slade. I don't know how, but I've got to do it."

Brian cheered. "Way to go, Dad! Lassie and Rin

Tin Tin wouldn't give up! Want a bowl of milk before you go?"

"No time, son. Get me my hat and trench coat, will you?"

"Sure," Brian hurried toward the closet, stopping at the window long enough to check the scene outside.

"Boy, Dad! A lot of policemen are talking with Admiral Brenner. I think the S.W.A.T. team is coming up. Hey! There's an officer headed over here!"

"Hurry with the coat and hat, Brian," Wilby called, giving Betty a quick kiss on the cheek.

The trench coat proved to be a little long, but the porkpie hat set off Wilby's shaggy ears perfectly.

"So long, honey."

"Good luck," Betty reached down and patted his head.

"Hurry, Pop. Hurry!" Brian handed him a pipe. "Just in case you need it," he said.

"Thanks, Brian. Look after your mother now."

"I will."

Wilby stood up on his hind legs and gave Betty a big hug. Then out the window he went, just as a knock sounded at the front door.

"*Yee-oh*, Dad!" Brian called softly after his father while Betty went to the door.

"Good evening, ma'am. There's a mad dog around—"

"Mad dog!" Betty stared. "Oh, I don't think he's—"

Brian pushed in front of his mother. "Yeah? What's he mad about?"

Before the officer finished the story, Wilby was safely out of reach—at least for a while!

11

TIM, once again in his ice cream truck, drove slowly up and down his usual selling route. "Maybe Elwood has come back to a neighborhood he knows. I'll look around, anyhow."

Turning into Brian Daniels' street, he saw the hub-bub going on in front of Admiral Brenner's house. He slowed down and parked. "Maybe they're looking for Elwood, too. After all, he *was* driving."

But after his experience in the police station, he decided not to get too close. He parked down the block, and then hugging the shrubbery, walked along the other side of the street. Suddenly, he was jerked back into the bushes and flattened on the ground. He looked up into a shaggy face beneath a porkpie hat.

. "Not a peep out of you!" Wilby's paws pinned

him tightly to the grass.

"Not a peep," Tim whispered. "Elwood, I've been looking for you everywhere."

"That's what I want to talk about," Wilby whispered back. "I may *look* like Elwood, but I'm not Elwood. I'm Wilby Daniels."

"Brian's father!" Tim gasped. "He usually takes vanilla."

"Forget vanilla," Wilby commanded. "Look. I'll take this from the top."

Carefully, he explained the theft of the Borgia ring from the Prescott Museum. Even more carefully, he explained his troubles from years before when he was a teenager. "So you see, Tim," he wound up, "Slade got hold of the ring. Now he's trying to win and get me out of the race—*really* out. I mean forever."

Tim's head whirled. He hadn't liked a thing he'd heard. It was too mixed up. If Elwood wasn't Elwood, where was Elwood? If Mr. Daniels wasn't really Elwood, how could a contract ever be signed for Tim and his Talking Dog?

"Is it all clear?" Wilby asked.

Tim swallowed. "Couldn't we just go back to selling ice cream and pies, Elwood? I mean, Mr. Daniels? I mean—Elwood?"

Wilby patted Tim's arm. "We'll get that settled later. Right now, I have to get Slade and Eddie Roschak before they get me. And you can help me, Tim."

Tim froze. "Fast Eddie Roschak, the crime boss? Oh, I don't think so, Mr. Daniels."

"You want Elwood back, don't you?"

"Oh, yes!"

"Then help me now."

"What do I got to do?"

Wilby's voice dropped almost below a whisper. "Well—I'll tell you . . ."

When the door closed on the departing policeman, Brian went to the window to keep an eye on the police activity next door. Admiral Brenner was stomping about and waving his arms toward his ruined Fluffy Ruffles petunias.

"Brian," Betty said. "I'm going into your father's den and work on his acceptance speech—just in case. I certainly hope he can go to the polls on Election Day. He needs every vote he can get."

"Yeah. Okay, Mom. Gosh! Admiral Brenner sure is mad about his flowers. I don't think we'd better tell him Dad did it."

"Goodness, no! Never mention it, Brian. We want to keep on good terms with the neighbors."

She left the room and Brian took up his watch at the window again. Under a street light, a bicycle rider with a passenger on the handlebars came gliding by. The rider wore a porkpie hat, a trench coat, and clenched a pipe between his teeth. The passenger wore the familiar Dolly Dixon uniform.

"Evening, officer," Brian heard his father call out.

"Move along." The officer waved his arm. "No slowing down. We want to keep this street clear."

"Yes, sir!" Wilby pedaled faster.

Brian waited only long enough to see which way his father turned at the corner. Then whipping out into the kitchen, he picked up his skateboard and let himself quietly out the back door.

The further from his ice cream truck Tim went, the more uneasy he became about the mission he was sharing with Wilby. He held tight to the handlebars and tried to keep his legs from getting involved with the front wheel. "Maybe you ought to look for someone else to help you, Elwood. I gotta get up early, and if I don't get my sleep, I—"

Wilby interrupted. "There *is* no one else, and there's no time. And I'm *not* Elwood."

Tim sighed. "Okay, Elwood. Where're we going?"

"*You're* going," Wilby answered. "Right into that house up ahead. You're going to beard the lion in his den—John Slade, himself. Remember, you want Elwood back."

Tim nearly shook himself off the handlebars. "What do I gotta do?"

"Just hold on steady. I'll explain. First you ring the doorbell. Then . . ."

When John Slade yanked open his front door, a tough-looking mug wearing a trench coat and porkpie hat gave him a shove in the chest. "You Slade?"

"I am," Slade bit out. "Who are you? And watch your manners!"

"Never mind dat. I got a message for ya from Fast Eddie. See? You're off the gravy train. Got it?" Tim gave Slade's chest another tap. "No more gravy."

He turned on his heel and marched off into the

darkness, leaving a worried John Slade behind him.

"Did he buy it?" Wilby asked, stepping out from behind a bush.

"I don't know dat. See?" Tim answered.

Wilby gave him a shake. "Don't say 'dat,' say 'that.' You can stop being a mug."

"Oh. Good." Tim sighed heavily and relaxed. "Now can I go back to my truck?"

Wilby didn't seem to hear. "If I've got Slade pegged right, he'll go straight over to Roschak's warehouse and we're going to be there."

Tim tottered. "Aw, Elwood. *Please.* I feel sorta sick. I ought to be home in bed."

"Hop on," Wilby said sternly. "There's no time to lose."

Following his father and Tim, Brian coasted around the corner of a building across the street from a warehouse. "Gosh," he muttered as he spotted Wilby and Tim go over a high fence into the warehouse grounds, "if I'd known Dad and Tim were going there I could have taken a shortcut I know. That place sure looks spooky to me."

Tim was thinking the same thing. The annex and big main building with its painted-over windows loomed bare and dismal in the moonlight. "I don't think we'll find the door open, Elwood," he quaked. "Maybe there's nobody home."

Wilby backed off to get a better look at the two buildings. "*Mmm.* Maybe we can get in through that skylight window on the roof."

"On the roof!" Tim gulped. "How'd we get all the way up there?"

Wilby pointed. "We go up that ladder along

that pipe over there, see? Then we cross over from one roof to the other one where the skylight is. They can't be thirty feet apart."

"Thirty feet! Elwood, I could never jump that far and neither could you."

"We won't have to. And STOP calling me 'Elwood.' You're not going to get Elwood back until we get that ring." Wilby studied the layout. "See that big connecting pipe up on top between the buildings? We'll cross on that."

Tim gasped. "Elwood—you lost your *mind*? You know I get dizzy. Don't you remember when we first got the ice cream truck I had to get used to being up so high?"

Wilby gave him a strong nudge toward the ladder. "Nonsense! You'll be great. Look what a great job you did with Slade."

For a moment, Tim looked pleased. "I was pretty good, I guess," he said modestly.

"Okay, then. You go first. I'll be right behind you."

Tim hung back. "I better stay here and keep a lookout."

Wilby bounced over and got a hold on a rung of the ladder. He lumbered up. "See, Tim? It's easy. Now, come ON."

Trembling, Tim followed.

In the shadows, Brian couldn't see where his father and Tim had gone. He coasted out on the skateboard, and noted his bike parked against a wire mesh fence. "They can't be far," he muttered. "Now which way to go?" He gave a couple of sharp whistles. "Here, Dad! Here, Dad!"

No reply. Resting his skateboard beside the bike, he began climbing the fence. At the top, he had a good view of the warehouse and annex. And there, high in the moonlight, a bulky, slow movement caught his eye. He looked harder. Far above the ground, he glimpsed his father and Tim moving along a big pipelike crossover.

"How'd they get up there?" he gasped. He lost no time in finding out.

Inching along, belly down, Wilby led the way. "Just don't look toward the ground, Tim. You'll be fine."

Tim, almost too frozen to move, clutched the big pipe with arms and legs. "You sure about that, Elwood?"

Wilby reached the down-curve where the pipe bent into the next roof. He took the slide, got to his feet and turned back to help Tim. "You're almost there, Tim. Keep coming."

Tim reached the down-curve. "Just slide," Wilby urged. "There's nothing to it."

Tim slid—right on his head. *Thumpp*!

"*Ssh!* These men are killers!" Wilby whispered.

Tim stumbled to his knees, rubbing his head. He looked back at the distance he had traveled and instantly clutched his arms around Wilby's shaggy neck. "And here they come! They're after us—*running*!"

Wilby looked up. "It's *Brian*!" he said hoarsely. "Don't say anything. It will distract him."

Brian sprinted along as though he'd spent his entire life practicing pipe-runs—and with no net.

Even a last-minute stumble didn't bother him. But Wilby's heart almost stopped beating. *"Brian, look out!"*

"Hi, Dad," called his son, getting his balance and answering cheerfully at the same time. He sprinted to the curve. "Here I come!"

Wilby held out his paws as Brian leaped forward. "I thought I told you to stay home and look after your mother," Wilby said, stern but trembling. He gave Brian a shaggy hug.

"Oh, Mom's okay. She's writing your acceptance speech. I can't give her any help on that, so I came to help you. Mom wants you home to go to the polls on Election Day. What're we doing way up here, anyhow?"

"Ssh. Talk low. I think this place is the center of a theft ring. And I think Slade is in on it."

"He thinks Slade's going to be here, too, with that ring I bought," Tim added helpfully. "And now, Mr. Daniels, now that your kid's here, you won't be needing me. Just keep Elwood at your house when you get yourself back to being you instead of Elwood. I'll be glad to pick him up there."

"Do you want to leave the way you got over, or would you rather go out the front door, Tim?" Wilby asked.

"Oh, the front door!" Tim replied with a shiver.

"Then follow me," Wilby ordered.

He pushed the open skylight wider, and one after another, the three slid through. Then stepping from one layer of big packing cases to the next, they safely reached the ground floor.

"Gosh!" Tim whispered. "This place looks like a big cave. There's only one little light going!"

"It's a big cave with a lot of furniture," Brian whispered back. He pointed along a long row of stolen refrigerators, stoves, TVs and stereo sets. "I bet they got our furniture here, Dad!" He stepped over to a TV-stereo. "Hey, look! Isn't this ours?"

Tim reached out and touched the tuning knob. *Plunk!* It fell and rolled on the floor.

"That's ours," Wilby sighed. He looked around. Down at the end of the aisle, a sliver of light shone beneath a door. "Come on. This way. No noise, now." He trundled ahead, paws making soft thuds on the concrete floor, but waited for Brian to turn the doorknob, slowly and quietly.

They peered in. "Look at the cars!" Brian gasped.

"Stolen cars," Wilby said. "This is where they do new paint jobs. This is some big operation Roschak has going here!"

"Is our car here, Dad?"

"It was probably sold the day after they painted it," Wilby replied sadly. "A great car like that would have moved fast."

The sound of a door opening made the trio duck back behind an inky black limousine. They heard two sets of footsteps striking on a metal staircase.

Eddie Roschak, followed by a man wearing paint-stained overalls, stopped halfway down the steps. "Paint it, then change the serial number like usual, Joe." He looked over the car tops. "We could use some Porsches. Tell the guys to keep their eyes open."

"We already got some spotted. Well, I'll close up, Mr. Roschak."

"You do that, Joe." Roschak turned and climbed back up the stairs. The door swung shut behind him. Joe let himself out through a door near the big drive-in entrance doors.

"Did you hear that, Dad?" Brian whispered. "You could bust him any time, *easy*."

Wilby shook his head. "It wouldn't prove Slade is in on this. I have to have proof." He glanced around the stacks of cartons, and stood stock-still, staring.

"I don't think Mr. Slade's in one of those, Dad," Brian said, puzzled.

"I don't think so either, Brian. But just *maybe*—. Tim, open that top carton, will you?"

"Sure." Tim popped one end and carefully shook out a small tape recorder.

"That could do it!" Wilby exclaimed eagerly. "We have to get it in Roschak's office somehow."

"How do you work it?" Brian asked, leaning over trying to read the buttons in the dim light.

"I think you just push this button here," said Tim, promptly doing so.

A blast of "The Stars and Stripes Forever" blared out. All three made a frantic grab to silence it. It spun to the floor and Wilby quick-wittedly punched the right button to OFF by sitting on all of them at once. "Hope Roschak didn't hear that!" he whispered.

Tim looked thoughtful. "I think it was the U. S. Marine Band."

"What are you going to do now, Dad?"

"Get it into Roschak's office, somehow." Wilby seized it in his jaws, started forward then ducked back at the sound of a door opening at the very end of the huge room.

"It's the night watchman—I think," Tim murmured. "He's sitting down. Oh! I think he's sitting down for *dinner*."

"You've got to move him away from there," Wilby growled. "He's right between me and Roschak's stairway."

"I—I wouldn't like to interrupt him on his break," Tim said earnestly. "Maybe later."

"Now!" Wilby said firmly. He gave Tim a push.

It wasn't easy for Tim to carry out this assignment. "Maybe I'd better be a mug again," he muttered uneasily, as he tiptoed along toward the night watchman's midnight snack. "My, but that salami does look good. Perhaps he'll offer me a slice."

All thoughts of salami fled from Tim's mind. His heart leaped as he saw a king-size knife blade flip open. He spun around—fast.

Wilby batted his paw. Plain as talking, it meant, "Back! Go back!"

Back went Tim. He marched right up to the watchman, his steps suddenly loud. "The *shanisfran* on the *rectafranser's* condensing," he muttered in his toughest voice.

"What—who—who are you?" The watchman jumped up.

"Roschak's new guy," Tim answered, rather liking the sound he was making. "It looks like it could *faflentehausen* the alternator, and somebody could slip in. Come on. I'll show you."

Brave as he had felt a moment before, Tim's legs wobbled as he led the watchman back toward Wilby. He managed, though, to keep up a stream of doubletalk that kept the watchman interested. They stopped between a row of stacked crates. Tim pointed. "Back in there. You'll have to bend down to see it."

Wilby, at this point, took future problems off Tim's shoulders in order to place them on the watchman's head. His shaggy paw gently edged over to a crate marked FM/AM. It tipped.

"Clunk!"

For the time being, the watchman took a well-earned rest.

Wilby bounced down, tape recorder still in his jaws. He raced toward the metal staircase, but slowed to tiptoe up the steps and carefully open the door. Roschak sat at a desk, busily counting out stacks of money and putting them into different envelopes.

Silently, Wilby glided his shaggy bulk to a chair behind Medfield's crime boss. Dropping the tape recorder on a padded chair, he put his large shaggy paw over the record button. To his relief, the tape started moving—and the U. S. Marine Band did NOT blare out.

With a muffled sigh, Wilby left—on tippy-toe and *fast*.

12

NO SOONER had Wilby safely cleared Fast Eddie Roschak's office than a buzzer sounded behind him. Hastily, he looked back in time to see him push a button on the desk. Slade's voice filled the room. "It's me. Let me in."

Wilby took a quick look around. "I can't risk meeting him on the stairs," he muttered. "Where'll I hide?"

He ducked under the secretary's desk, made himself small as possible, and hoped his tail wasn't showing from the entrance door. He needn't have worried. Slade burst in, strode rapidly past Wilby's hideout, and on up to Roschak's desk.

Wilby had a good view of the two men. Roschak stared coldly at the D. A. "This ain't very smart, Slade, you coming here."

Slade's eyes flew sparks. "If you've any ideas about cutting me out, I want it right from you, not one of your messenger boys."

Fast Eddie's eyebrows rose. "I don't know what you're talking about."

"No? I suppose you don't know one of your punks came to my house tonight and started leaning on me—and I quote, 'you're off the gravy train.' "

Roschak looked puzzled. "I still don't know what you're talking about. It's business as usual with us, John."

Wilby noted with satisfaction that the little tape recorder was getting down some very interesting conversation.

Slade spoke again. "Then if you didn't send him, who did?"

"Beats me. But I'll find out, and when I do, he gets scratched—permanent. Might have been that stupid Daniels. But he's gotta have evidence in court, right? He's a lawyer. He oughtta know that."

He stood up and walked around the desk. "Look, Slade, I was just ready to close up here for the night. We can go downstairs together."

Wilby's brain raced. If he didn't move fast, he'd never get the tape recorder. Worse, he might be locked in the office for the night. With a giant bound, he raced forward, grabbed the tape recorder in his mouth, spun around and galloped to the outer door.

"How'd that dog get in here?" he heard Roschak gasp.

"It's him! That's Daniels!" Honest John yelled.

"Get him! He's taped the whole thing!"

"That's Daniels?"

Wilby raced down the stairs, Slade shrieking behind him. "Don't ask questions. Shoot him!"

There was a deafening report as a bullet slammed into a huge TV screen. Slade and Roschak dived for safety. Glass splinters flew everywhere.

Wilby never moved so fast in his life—not even in the Rollerdrome. He went skidding up to Brian and Tim's hiding place. It was tough talking with a tape recorder in his mouth, but the message was clear enough. "Take this. Get out of here. I'll draw them off. Grab one of those cars and get going!"

He dashed into the open, *woof-woofing* loudly. It wasn't too good.

"Woof?" Roschak repeated.

"Forget that!" Slade commanded. "Just *shoot!*"

As the two galloped off, hot on Wilby's trail, Brian yanked and pulled the terrified Tim into action. Unseen by Fast Eddie and Honest John, they headed for the garage.

To Wilby's despair, although he succeeded in heading off the enemy, his hasty flight had trapped him in a dead-end of chairs, sofas, desks, tables, and more chairs—and Slade had him spotted.

"Daniels! Come on out. Let's get this over with. You don't have a chance. I've got the ring and you've got nothing. Come out!"

Horror-stricken, Wilby saw Honest John whirl and snatch the gun from Roschak.

"Goodbye Betty! Goodbye Brian!" he groaned. "Remember—I *tried* to clean up Medfield."

"YEE-OH!" Wilby couldn't believe his ears. He

looked up toward the skylight. With the wild sound of attacking cavalry, his dog friends from the pound came streaming down, leaping from crate to crate, barreling along straight for Slade and Roschak.

Working as a team, Jimmy and Bogie slammed Slade off his feet. The scarab ring went flying. Like lightning, Jimmy snapped it mid-air. "Hey! This what you're looking for, pal?" he asked Wilby.

"That's it! Thanks. Thanks. You've no idea what you've done for me, fellas."

Bogie shrugged. "Forget it. It's on us, sweetheart."

"We take care of our own, see?" Eddie grinned.

It was no grin for Roschak. Snapping teeth yanked him back to the floor. Peter, the dignified setter, gave them both a dirty look. Then, with an expert hind-leg kick, he belted Roschak's gun into the jungle of chair legs.

The whole thing lasted only moments. "S'long, pal," Mae called softly. "It's goodbye-time, handsome. We gotta split."

Fast as they had spilled down from the skylight, Wilby's faithful friends went scrambling up and out of sight.

Stunned, Wilby held the ring in his paw. He stared. "Hands! I'm getting *hands* again!"

With a wild, delighted cry, he hopped over the fallen foe and made it to the garage. Behind him, Roschak wriggled between chair legs, and wriggled back with the gun. "Which way, Slade?" he gasped.

Honest John yanked him to his feet. "The garage! Fast! That bum! He's *stealing* one of our cars, I'll bet."

They rushed into the garage just in time to see Wilby and Brian, with Tim behind the wheel of a jeep, head for the drive-in doors.

"Stop him!" Slade screeched.

Roschak opened fire. Tim zoomed into a U-turn. Slade jumped up and down, shouting his rage. Brian hung on to the tape recorder and Wilby hung on to the ring.

Only Tim looked calm and pleased. "I think Katrinka would like this jeep," he said approvingly. "Wait 'til—" The rest of his words were lost as he wheeled sharply. The jeep sailed through the paint booth. It, and the occupants, speedily emerged —bright tangerine orange. Tim sputtered, and made a sharp turn straight into a stack of mattresses and pillows dead ahead. He gunned the motor— and a blizzard of feathers exploded into the air. For a moment, the garage looked almost beautiful as soft, downy feathers drifted over everything and everybody.

Full speed, Tim, now clad in tangerine-colored feathers, zoomed out the garage doors and past Raymond, who was peering from behind the wheel of Slade's limousine. To Raymond's amazement, his employer leaped out from the warehouse, wearing what seemed to be a complete feather outfit.

Slade jerked open the door and hurled himself into the back.

"What was that?" Raymond asked stupidly.

"Daniels, you ninny! Get after him!"

The wildly colored jeep went bounding down the avenue and through an intersection just as the signal light was flipping from yellow to red.

"What was *that*?" the driver of a patrol car asked his partner.

Before there was an answer, Slade's black limousine came pouring fast as ink under the red light. The patrol car swept out from the curb, siren wailing.

"He's got us, boss," Raymond said, pulling to a stop.

"Tell him who I am, and that it's official business," Slade snapped. "*In Canis Corpore Transmuto*," he muttered—almost from habit, as he had been saying that all evening.

Both cops strode over to the limousine. "Officer," Raymond said, "District Attorney John Slade's back there, and we're on official business."

The officer flashed a light to the back seat. "Is he now? I don't see him."

Raymond turned. To his horror, the back seat was occupied only by an English bulldog, chewing on a cigar and clutching a brief case!

Up ahead, Tim careened around a corner, expecting Slade to crowd them to the curb any second. "Stop!" Wilby yelled, spotting a policeman walking his beat. "Officer!" he shouted, as Tim screeched the brakes. He held out the tape recorder. "Hang on to this, and don't let anybody touch it till the grand jury hears it."

"Yeah," Tim yelled out importantly. "Or it will mean your badge!"

They zoomed off, heading for home—at last.

Midway along Wilby's block was the ice cream truck, and patiently waiting in the passenger seat was Elwood.

"Elwood! Elwood! It's you! It's me! Oh, this is wonderful, Mr. Daniels. I'll say s'long, now. See you on Election Day!"

Betty opened the front door and stared at the strange pair grinning at her.

"Hey, Mom—we're home!" Brian exclaimed. "Pop's not a dog anymore."

"Wilby! Brian! Oh darlings! For a minute I thought it was Trick or Treat." She threw her arms around them both, slapping smack into paint and feathers.

"Birds of a feather flock together," Brian called out from somewhere under his parents loving wings. "I heard that somewhere," he added, in a muffled voice. "And Dad, you better get rid of that ring FOREVER!"

It was a Wilby Daniels landslide! And only a few days later, the Medfield *Bugle* front-paged the story of Honest John Slade's and Fast Eddie Roschak's appearance in court. Betty read the story aloud to Wilby and Brian as they drove along Medfield's main street in Wilby's new car.

"Listen to this. 'Slade's successor, Wilby Daniels, who risked his life to get evidence, will testify before the grand jury.' Brian, you and Tim are mentioned here, too."

"Hey, look!" Brian yelled. "There's Tim and Miss Muggelberg coming out of the deli."

Wilby swung over to the curb. "How's the going, pardner?" he called.

"We're shopping for our engagement party," Katrinka beamed.

Prancing out around the pair came Elwood. Following him, on a long leash, were all of Wilby's friends from the pound.

"My gang!" Wilby cried out.

"Your what, dear?" Betty asked.

A sudden sadness welled up in Wilby's heart. Happy small yaps, friendly big and little woofs— he knew he'd never hear a *word* again. He reached into his billfold. "Here, Tim. Take this, will you? It's for the gang."

Tim looked down at the folded money. His eyes widened. "Sure will, Mr. D. A." he grinned. "Katrinka, jot down porterhouse steaks. Better make it sixteen."

"See you at the party," Betty waved as Wilby began to slide the car forward.

The gang watched. "Now there's my kind of people!" Jimmy exclaimed.

Eddie nodded. "Yeah, ya feel like somehow they *understand*.

Mae only sighed, her brown eyes loving and tender.

At that moment, Wilby glanced back. Bogie perked up one ear and waggled it at Wilby. And Wilby *did* understand! He almost heard the words —"So if you want anything, sweetheart—just whistle!"